ALSO BY GREG BEAR
Published by ibooks, inc.:

Blood Music
Strength of Stones

ABOUT THE AUTHOR

GREG BEAR is the author of over twenty-seven books of science fiction and fantasy. He has been awarded two Hugo and five Nebula Awards for his fiction, one of two authors to win a Nebula in every category. He has been called the "best working writer of science fiction" by *The Ultimate Encyclopedia of Science Fiction*. His novel *Darwin's Radio*, published by Ballantine Books, won the Nebula Award for "Best Novel of 2000," and was honored with the prestigious Endeavor Award. His most recent novel is *Vitals*, published in January 2002 by Del Ray. He is married to Astrid Anderson Bear. They are the parents of two children, Erik and Alexandra.

W³

WOMEN IN DEEP TIME

GREG BEAR

ibooks
new york
www.ibooks.net

DISTRIBUTED BY SIMON & SCHUSTER, INC.

INTRODUCTION

These three stories have a theme in common: the female psyche, multiplied and divided. There's probably something Jungian in common with all three. At any rate, throughout my writing career (and for whatever reason) I've been fascinated by the feminine voice.

"Sisters" was commissioned by Brian Thomsen at Warner Books to finish off an anthology published in 1989.

"Scattershot" was written on spec and published by Terry Carr in his anthology *Universe 8* in 1978.

Hardfought was published in early 1983, almost simultaneously, in *Isaac Asimov's Science Fiction Magazine* (edited by Shawna McCarthy) and in my first collection, *The Wind from a Burning Woman*, edited by James Turner.

I still like to write about women. Some of my novels featuring strong females are *Beyond Heaven's River*, *Strength of Stones*, *Eon*, *Eternity*, *Queen of Angels*, *Slant*, *Moving Mars*, *Darwin's Radio*, and *Darwin's Children*.

Dinosaur Summer, a boy's adventure story populated almost entirely by males, was chastised by one critic for not having a strong and prominent female character.

Mea maxima culpa.

But it did. Two, in fact.

Both dinosaurs.

Is it possible for a man or woman to write across gender lines, and be convincing? Of course.

I don't take much of the modern gender nonsense very seriously. My attitude is pretty radical.

I think we're all different sexes, inside.

—Greg Bear
August 2002

SISTERS

But you're the only one, Letitia." Reena Cathcart lay a light, slender hand on her shoulder with a look of utmost sincerity. "You know none of the others can. I mean . . ." She stopped, the slightest hint of awareness of her *faux pas* dawning. "You're simply the only one who can play the old—the older—woman."

Letitia Blakely looked down at the hall floor, eyes and face hot, then circled her gaze up to the ceiling, trying to keep the fresh tears from spilling over. Reena tossed her long black hair, perfect hazel eyes imploring. A few stragglers sauntered down the clean and carpeted hall of the new school wing to their classes. "We're late for first period," Letitia said. "Why the old woman? Why didn't you come to me when there was some other part to play?"

Reena was too smart not to know what she was doing. Smart, but not terribly sensitive. "You're the type."

2

"You mean frowsy?"

Reena didn't react. She was intent on a yes answer, the perfect solution to her problems.

"Or just dumpy?"

"You shouldn't be ashamed of how you look."

"I look frowsy and *dumpy!* I'm perfect for the old woman in your lysing play, and you're the only one with the guts to ask me."

"We'd like to give you a chance. You're such a loner, and we want you to feel like you're part—"

"Bullmusk!" The moisture spilled over and Reena backed away. "Leave me alone. Just leave me alone."

"No need to swear." Petulant, offended.

Letitia raised her hand as if to strike. Reena swung her hair again defiantly and turned to walk away. Letitia leaned against the tile wall and wiped her eyes, trying to avoid damage to her carefully applied makeup. The damage was already done, however. She could feel the tear-tracks of her mother's mascara and the smudged eyeshadow. With a sigh, she walked off to the bathroom, not caring how late she was. She wanted to go home.

Coming into class fifteen minutes after the bell, Letitia was surprised to find the students in self-ordered discussion, with no sign of Mr. Brant. Several of Reena's drama group gave her frosty looks as she took her seat.

"TB," Edna Corman said beneath her breath from across the aisle.

"RC you," Letitia replied, head cocked to one side and tone matching Edna' s precisely. She poked John

Lockwood in the shoulder. Lockwood didn't much care for socializing; he seldom noticed the exchanges going on around him. "Where's Mr. Brant?"

"Georgia Fischer blitzed and he took her to the counselors. He told us to plug in and pursue."

"Oh." Georgia Fischer had transferred two months ago from a superwhiz class in Oakland. She was brighter than most but she blitzed about once every two weeks. "I may be fat and ugly," Letitia said for Lockwood's ears only. "But I never blitz."

"Nor I," Lockwood said. He was PPC, like Georgia, but not a superwhiz. Letitia liked him, but not enough to feel threatened by him. "Better pursue."

Letitia leaned back in her seat and closed her eyes to concentrate. Her mod activated and projections danced in front of her, then steadied. She had been cramming patient psych for a week and was approaching threshold. The little Computer Graphics nursie in whites and pillcap began discussing insanouts of terminal patient care, which all seemed very TB to Letitia; who died of disease now, anyway? She made her decision and cut to the same CG nursie discussing the shock of RoR—replacement and recovery. What she really wanted to study was colony medicine, but how could she ever make it Out There?

Some PPCs had been designed by their parents to qualify physically and mentally for space careers. Some had been equipped with bichemistries, one of which became active in Earth's gravity, the other in space. How could an NG compete with that?

Of the seven hundred adolescents in her high school training programs, Letitia Blakely was one of ten NGs—possessors of natural, unaltered genomes. Everyone else was the proud bearer of juggled genes, PPCs or Pre-Planned Children, all lovely and stable with just the proper amount of adipose tissue and just the proper infusion of parental characteristics and chosen features to be beautiful and different; tall, healthy, hair manageable, skin unblemished, well-adjusted (except for the occasional blitzer) with warm and sunny personalities. The old derogatory slang for PPCs was RC—Recombined.

Letitia, slightly overweight, skin pasty, hair frizzy, bulbous-nosed and weak-chinned, one breast larger than the other and already showing a droop pronounced enough to grip a stylus—with painful menstrual periods and an absolute indisposition to athletics—was the Sport. That's what they were called. NG Sports. TBs—Throwbacks. Neanderthals.

All the beautiful PPCs risked a great deal if they showed animosity toward the NGs. Her parents had the right to sue the system if she was harassed to the detriment of her schooling. This wasn't a private school where all parents paid astronomical tuitions; this was an old-fashioned public school, with public school programs and regulations. Teachers tended to nuke out on raggers. And, she admitted to herself with a painful loop of recrimination, she wasn't making it any easier for them.

Sure, she could join in, play the old woman—how much realism she would contribute to their little drama, with her genuine TB phys! She could be jolly and self-deprecating like Helen Roberti, who wasn't all that bad-looking anyway—she could pass if she straightened her hair. Or she could be quiet and camouflaged like Bernie Thibhault.

The CG nursie exited from RoR care. Letitia had hardly absorbed a thing. Realtime mod education was a bore, but she hadn't yet qualified for experience training. She had only one course of career study now—no alternates—and two aesthetic programs, individual orchestra on Friday afternoon and LitVid publishing on alternating weekends.

For pre-med, she was a washout, but she wouldn't admit it. She was NG. Her brain took longer to mature; it wasn't as finely wired.

She thought she was incredibly slow. She doubted whether she would ever be successful as a doctor; she was squeamish, and nobody, not even her fellow NGs, would want to be treated by a doctor who grew pale at the sight of blood.

Letitia silently told nursie to start over again, and nursie obliged.

Reena Cathcart, meanwhile, had dropped into her mod with a vengeance. Her blissed expression told it all. The realtime ed slid into her so smooth, so quick, it was pure joy.

No zits on her brain.

Mr. Brant returned ten minutes later with a pale and bleary-eyed Georgia Fischer. She sat two seats behind Letitia and over one aisle. She plugged in her mod dutifully and Brant went to his console to bring up the multimedia and coordinate the whole class. Edna Corman whispered something to her.

"Not a bad blitz, all in all," Georgia commented softly.

"How are you doing, Letitia?" the autocounselor asked. The CG face projected in front of her with some slight wirehash, which Letitia paid no attention to. CG ACs were the jams and she didn't appreciate them even in pristine perfection.

"Poorly," she said.

"Really? Care to elaborate?"

"I want to talk to Dr. Rutger."

"Don't trust your friendly AC?"

"I'd like some clear space. I want to talk to Dr. Rutger."

"Dr. Rutger is busy, dear. Unlike your friendly AC, humans can only be in one place at a time. I'd like to help if I may."

"Then I want program sixteen."

"Done, Letitia." The projection wavered and the face changed to a real-person simulation of Marian Tempesino, the only CG AC Letitia felt comfortable with.

Tempesino had no wirehash, which indicated she was a seldom-used program, and that was just fine with Letitia. "Sixteen here. Letitia? You're looking cut. More adjustment jams?"

"I wanted to talk with Dr. Rutger but he's busy. So I'll talk to you. And I want it on my record. I want out of school. I want my parents to pull me and put me in a special NG school."

Tempesino's face didn't wear any particular expression, which was one of the reasons Letitia liked Program 16 AC. "Why?"

"Because I'm a freak. My parents made me a freak and I'd like to know why I shouldn't be with all the other freaks."

7

"You're a natural, not a freak."

"To look like any of the others even to look like Reena Cathcart—I'd have to spend the rest of my life in bioplasty. I can't take it anymore. They asked me to play an old lady in one of their dramas. The only part I'm fit for. An old lady."

"They tried to include you in."

"That hurt!" Letitia said, tears in her eyes.

Tempesino's image wavered a bit as the emotion registered and a higher authority AC kicked in behind 16.

"I just want out. I want to be alone."

"Where would you like to go, Letitia?"

Letitia thought about it for a moment. "I'd like to go back to when being ugly was normal."

"Fine, then. Let's simulate. Sixty years should do it. Ready?"

She nodded and wiped away more mascara with the back of her hand.

"Then let's go."

It was like a dream, somewhat fuzzier than plugging in a mod. CG images compiled from thousands of miles of old films and tapes and descriptive records made her feel as if she were flying back in time, back to a place she would have loved to call home. Faces came to her— faces with ugly variations, growing old prematurely, wearing glasses, even beautiful faces which could have passed today—and the faces pulled away to become attached to bodies. Bodies out of shape, in good condition, overweight, sick and healthy, red-faced with high blood pressure: the whole variable and disaster-prone

8

population of humanity, sixty years past. This was where Letitia felt she belonged.

"They're beautiful," she said.

"They didn't think so. They jumped at the chance to be sure their children were beautiful, smart, and healthy. It was a time of transition, Letitia. Just like now."

"Everybody looks alike now."

"I don't think that's fair," the AC said. "There's a considerable variety in the way people look today."

"Not my age."

"Especially your age. Look." The AC showed her dozens of faces. Few looked alike, but all were handsome or lovely. Some made Letitia ache; faces she could never be friends with, never love, because there was always someone more beautiful and desirable than an NG.

"My parents should have lived back then. why did they make me a freak?"

"You're developmentally normal. You're not a freak."

"Sure. I'm a DNG. Dingy. That's what they call me."

"Don't you invite the abuse sometimes?"

"No!" This was getting her nowhere.

"Letitia, we all have to adjust. Not even today's world is fair. Are you sure you're doing all you can to adjust?"

Letitia squirmed in her seat and said she wanted to leave. "Just a moment," the AC said. "We're not done yet." she knew that tone of voice. The ACs were allowed to get a little rough at times. They could make unruly

9

students do grounds duty or detain them after hours to work on assignments usually given to computers. Letitia sighed and settled back. She hated being lectured.

"Young woman, you're carrying a giant chip on your shoulder."

"That's all the more computing capacity for me."

"Quiet, and listen. We're all allowed to criticize policy, whoever makes it. Dignity of office and respect for superiors has not survived very well into Century Twenty-one. People have to earn respect. That goes for students, too. The average student here has four major talents, each of them fitting into a public planning policy which guarantees them a job incorporating two or more of those talents. They aren't forced to accept the jobs, and if their will falters, they may not keep those jobs. But the public has tried to guarantee every one of us a quality employment opportunity. That goes for you, as well. You're DNG, but you also show as much intelligence and at least as many developable talents as the PPCs. You are young, and your maturation schedule is a natural one—but you are not inferior or impaired, Letitia. That's more than can be said for the offspring of some parents even more resistive than your own. you at least were given prenatal care and nutrition adjustment, and your parents let the biotechs correct your allergies."

"So?"

"So for you, it's all a matter of will. If your will falters, you won't be given any more consideration than a PPC. You'll have to choose secondary or tertiary employment, or even..." The AC paused. "Public support. Do you want that?"

"My grades are up. I'm doing fine."

"You are choosing career training not matching your developable talents."

"I like medicine."

"You're squeamish."

Letitia shrugged.

"And you're hard to get along with."

"Just tell them to lay off. I'll be civil . . . but I don't want them treating me like a freak. Edna Corman called me . . ." She paused. That could get Edna Corman into a lot of trouble. Among the students, TB was a casual epithet; to school authorities, applied to an NG, it might be grounds for a blot on Corman's record. "Nothing. Not important."

The AC switched to lower authority and Tempesino's face took a different counseling track. "Fine. Adjustment on both sides is necessary. Thank you for coming in, Letitia."

"Yeah. I still want to talk with Rutger."

"Request has been noted. Please return to your class in progress."

"Pay attention to your brother when he's talking," Jane said. Roald was making a nuisance of himself by chattering about the preflight training he was getting in primary. Letitia made a polite comment or two, then lapsed back into contemplation of the food before her. She didn't eat. Jane regarded her from the corner of her eye and passed a bowl of sugared berries. "What's eating you?"

"I'm doing the eating," Letitia said archly.

"Ha," Roald said. "Full load from this angle." He

grinned at her, his two front teeth missing. He looked hideous, she thought. Any other family would have given him temporaries; not hers.

"A little more respect from both of you," said Donald. Her father took the bowl from Roald and scooped a modest portion into his cup, then set it beside Letitia. "Big fifteen and big eight." That was his homily; behave big whether eight or fifteen.

"Autocounselor today?" Jane asked. She knew Letitia much too well.

"AC," Letitia affirmed.

"Did you go in?"

"Yes."

"And?"

"I'm not tuned."

"Which means?" Donald asked.

"It means she hisses and crackles," Roald said, mouth full of berries, juice dripping down his chin. He cupped his hand underneath and sucked it up noisily. Jane reached out and finished the job with a napkin. "She complains," Roald finished.

"About what?"

Letitia shook her head and didn't answer.

The dessert was almost finished when Letitia slapped both palms on the table. "Why did you do it?"

"Why did we do what?" he father asked, startled.

"Why are Roald and I normal? Why didn't you design us?"

Jane and Donald glanced at each other quickly and turned to Letitia. Roald regarded her with wide eyes, a bit shocked himself.

"Surely you know why by now," Jane said, looking

down at the table, either nonplussed or getting angry. Now that she had laid out her course, Letitia couldn't help but forge ahead.

"I don't. Not really. It's not because you're religious."

"Something like that," Donald said.

"No," Jane said, shaking her head firmly.

"Then why?"

"Your mother and I—"

"I am *not* just their mother," Jane said.

"Jane and I believe there is a certain plan in nature, a plan we shouldn't interfere with. If we had gone along with most of the others and tried to have PPCs— participated in the boy-girl lotteries and signed up for the pre-birth opportunity counseling— why, we would have been interfering."

"Did you go to a hospital when we were born?"

"Yes," Jane said, still avoiding their faces.

"That's not natural," Letitia said. "Why not let nature decide whether we'd be born alive?"

"We have never claimed to be consistent," Donald said.

"Donald," Jane said ominously.

"There are limits," Donald expanded, smiling placation. "We believe those limits begin when people try to interfere with the sex cells. You've had all that in school. You know about the protests when the first PPCs were born. Your grandmother was one of the protesters. Your mother and I are both NGs; of course, our generation has a much higher percentage of NGs."

"Now we're freaks," Letitia said.

"If by that you mean there aren't many teenage

NGs, I suppose that's right," Donald said, touching his wife's arm. "But it could also mean you're special. Chosen."

"No," Letitia said. "Not chosen. You played dice with both of us. We could have been DDs. Duds. Not just dingies, but retards or spaz."

An uncomfortable quiet settled over the table. "Not likely," Donald said, his voice barely above a whisper. "Your mother and I both have good genotypes. Your grandmother insisted your mother marry a good genotype. There are no developmentally disabled people in our families."

Letitia had been hemmed in. There was no way she could see out of it, so she pushed back her chair and excused herself from the table.

As she made her way up to her room, she heard arguing below. Roald raced up the stairs behind her and gave her a dirty look. "Why'd you have to bring all that up?" he asked. "It's bad enough at school, we don't have to have it here."

She thought about the history the AC had shown her. Back then, a family with their income wouldn't have been able to live in a four-bedroom house. Back then, there had been half as many people in the United States and Canada as there were now. There had been more unemployment, much more economic uncertainty, and far fewer automated jobs. The percentage of people doing physical labor for a living— simple construction, crop maintenance and harvesting, digging ditches and hard work like that— had been ten times greater then than it was now.

Most of the people doing such labor today belonged to religious sects or one of the Wendell Barry farming communes.

Back then, Roald and Letitia would have been considered gifted children with a bright future.

She thought about the pictures and the feeling of the past, and wondered if Reena hadn't been right.

She would be a perfect old woman.

Her mother came into her room while Letitia was putting up her hair. She stood in the doorframe. It was obvious she had been crying. Letitia watched her reflection in the mirror of her grandmother's dressing table, willed to her four years before. "Yes?" she asked softly, ageless bobby pins in her mouth.

"It was more my idea than your father's," Jane said, stepping closer, hands folded before her. "I mean, I am your mother. We've never really talked about this."

"No," Letitia said.

"So why now?"

"Maybe I'm growing up."

"Yes." Jane looked at the soft and flickering pictures hung on the walls, pastel scenes of improbable forests. "When I was pregnant with you, I was very afraid. I worried we'd made the wrong decision, going against what everybody else seemed to think and what everybody was advising or being advised. But I carried you and felt you move . . . and I knew you were ours, and ours alone, and that we were responsible for you body and soul. I was your mother, not the doctors."

15

Letitia looked up with mixed anger and frustration . . . and love.

"And now I see you. I think back to what I might have felt, if I were your age again, in your position. I might be mad, too. Roald hasn't had time to feel different yet; he's too young. I just came up here to tell you; I know that what I did was right, not for us, not for them"—she indicated the broad world beyond the walls of the house—"but right for you. It will work out. It really will." she put her hands on Letitia's shoulders. "They aren't having an easy time either. You know that." she stopped for a moment, then from behind her back revealed a book with a soft brown cover. "I brought this to show you again. You remember Great-Grandma? Her grandmother came all the way from Ireland, along with her grandpa." Jane gave her the album. Reluctantly, Letitia opened it up. There were real photographs inside, on paper, ancient black and white and faded color. Her great-grandmother did not much resemble Grandmother, who had been big-boned, heavy-set. Great-grandmother looked as if she had been skinny all her life. "You keep this," Jane said. "Think about it for a while."

The morning came with planned rain. Letitia took the half-empty metro to school, looking at the terraced and gardened and occasionally neglected landscape of the extended suburbs through raindrop-smeared glass. She came onto the school grounds and went to one of the older buildings in the school, where there was a little-used old-fashioned lavatory. This sometimes served as her sanctuary. She stood in a white stall and breathed deeply for a few minutes, then went to a sink and washed her hands as if conducting some ritual. Slowly, reluctantly, she looked at herself in the cracked mirror. A janitorial worker went about its duties, leaving behind the fresh, steamy smell of clean fixtures.

The early part of the day was a numb time. Letitia began to fear her own distance from feeling, from the people around her. She might at any minute step into the old lavatory and simply fade from the present, find herself sixty years back . . .

And what would she really think of that?

In her third period class she received a note requesting that she appear in Rutger's counseling office as soon as was convenient. That was shorthand for immediately; she gathered up her mods and caught Reena's unreadable glance as she walked past.

Rutger was a handsome man of forty-three (the years were registered on his desk life clock, an affectation of some of the older PPCs) with a broad smile and a garish taste in clothes. He was head of the counseling department and generally well-liked in the school. He shook her hand as she entered the counseling office and offered her a chair. "Now. You wanted to talk to me?"

"I guess," Letitia said.

"Problems?" His voice was a pleasant baritone; he was probably a fairly good singer. That had been a popular trait in the early days of PPCs.

"The ACs say it's my attitude."

"And what about it?"

"I . . . am ugly. I am the ugliest girl . . . the only girl in this school who is ugly."

Rutger nodded. "I don't think you're ugly, but which is worse, being unique or being ugly?" Letitia lifted the corner of one lip in snide acknowledgment of the funny.

"Everybody's unique now," she said.

"That's what we teach. Do you believe it?"

"No," she said. "Everybody's the same. I'm ..." She shook her head. She resented Rutger prying up the pavement over her emotions. "I'm TB. I wouldn't mind being a PPC, but I'm not."

"I think it's a minor problem," Rutger said quickly. He hadn't even sat down; obviously he was not going to give her much time.

"It doesn't feel minor," she said, anger poking through the cracks he had made.

"Oh, no. Being young often means that minor problems feel major. You feel envy and don't like yourself, at least not the way you look. Well, looks can be helped by diet, or at the very least by time. If I'm any judge, you'll look fine when you're older. And I am something of a judge. As for the way the others feel about you ... I was a freak once."

Letitia looked up at him.

"Certainly. Bona fide. Much more of a freak than you. There are ten NGs like yourself in this school now. When I was your age, I was the only PPC in my school. There was still suspicion and even riots. Some PPCs were killed in one school when parents stormed the grounds."

Letitia stared.

"The other kids hated me. I wasn't bad-looking, but they knew. They had parents who told them PPCs were Frankenstein monsters. Do you remember the Rifkin Society? They're still around, but they're extreme fringies now. Just as well. They thought I'd been grown in a test tube somewhere and hatched out of an incubator. You've never experienced real hatred, I suspect. I did."

"You were nice-looking," Letitia said. "You knew somebody would like you eventually, maybe even love you. But what about me? Because of what I am, the way I look, who will ever want me? And will a PPC ever want to be with a Dingy?"

She knew these were hard questions and Rutger made no pretense of answering them. "Say it all works out for the worst," he said. "You end up a spinster and no one ever loves you. you spend the rest of your days alone. Is that what you're worried about?"

Her eyes widened. She had never quite thought those things through. Now she really hurt.

"Everybody out there is choosing beauty for their kids. They're choosing slender, athletic bodies and fine minds. You have a fine mind, but you don't have an athletic body. Or so you seem to be convinced; I have no record of you ever trying out for athletics. So when you're out in the adult world, sure, you'll look different. But why can't that be an advantage? You may be surprised how hard we PPCs try to be different. And how hard it is, since tastes vary so little in our parents. You have that built in."

Letitia listened, but the layers of paving were closing again. "Icing on the cake," she said.

Rutger regarded her with his shrewd blue eyes and shrugged. "Come back in a month and talk to me," he said. "Until then, I think autocounselors will do fine."

Little was said at dinner and less after. She went upstairs and to bed at an early hour, feeling logy and hoping for escape.

Her father did his usual bedcheck an hour after she had put on her pajamas and lain down. "Rolled tight?" he asked.

"Mmph," she replied.

"Sleep tighter," he said. Rituals and formulas. Her life had been shaped by parents who were comfortable with nightly rituals and formulas.

Almost immediately after sleep, or so it seemed, she came abruptly awake. She sat up in bed and realized where she was, and who, and began to cry. She had had the strangest and most beautiful dream, the finest ever without a dream mod. She could not remember details now, try as she might, but waking was almost more than she could bear.

In first period, Georgia Fischer blitzed yet again and had to go to the infirmary. Letitia watched the others and saw a stony general cover-up of feelings. Edna Corman excused herself in second period and came back with red puffy eyes and pink cheeks. The tension built through the rest of the day until she wondered how anyone could concentrate. She did her own studying without any conviction; she was still wrapped in the dream, trying to decide what it meant.

In eighth period, she once again sat behind John Lockwood. It was as if she had completed a cycle beginning in the morning and ending with her last class. She looked at her watch anxiously. Once again, they had Mr. Brant supervising. He seemed distracted, as if he, too, had had a dream, and it hadn't been as pleasant as hers.

Brant had them cut mods mid-period and begin a discussion on what had been learned. These were the so-called integrative moments when the media learning was fixed by social interaction; Letitia found these periods a trial at the best of times. The others discussed their economics, Reena Cathcart as usual standing out in a class full of dominant personalities.

John Lockwood listened intently, a small smile on his face as he presented a profile to Letitia. He seemed about to turn around and talk to her. She placed her hand on the corner of her console and lifted her finger to attract his attention.

He glanced at her hand, turned away, and with a shudder looked at it again, staring this time, eyes widening. His mouth began to work as if her hand was the most horrible thing he had ever seen. His chin quivered, then his shoulder, and before Letitia could react he stood up and moaned. His legs went liquid beneath him and he fell to the console, arms hanging, then slid to the noor. On the floor, John Lockwood— who had never done such a thing in his life—twisted and groaned and shivered, locked in a violent blitz.

Brant pressed the class emergency button and came around his desk. Before he could reach Lockwood, the boy became still, eyes open, one hand letting go its tight grip on the leg of his seat. Letitia could not move, watching his empty eyes; he appeared so horribly *limp*.

Brant grabbed the boy by the shoulders, swearing steadily, and dragged him outside the classroom. Letitia followed them into the hall, wanting to help. Edna Corman and Reena Cathcart stood beside her, faces blank. Other students followed, staying well away from Brant and the boy.

Brant lowered John Lockwood to the concrete and began pounding his chest and administering mouth-to-mouth. He pulled a syringe from his coat pocket and uncapped it, shooting its full contents into the boy's skin just below the sternum. Letitia focused on the syringe, startled. Right in his pocket; not in the first aid kit.

The full class stood in the hallway, silent, in shock. The medical arrived, Rutger following; it scooped John Lockwood onto its gurney and swung around, lights flashing. "Have you administered KVN?" the robot asked Brant.

"Yes. Five cc's. Direct to heart."

Room after room came out to watch, all the PPCs fixing their eyes on the burdened medical as it rolled down the hall. Edna Corman cried. Reena glanced at Letitia and turned away as if ashamed.

"That's five," Rutger said, voice tired beyond grimness. Brant looked at him, then at the class, and told them they were dismissed. Letitia hung back. Brant screwed up his face in grief and anger. "Go! Get out of here!"

She ran. The last thing she heard Rutger say was, "More this week than last."

Letitia sat in the empty white lavatory, wiping her eyes, ashamed at her sniveling. She wanted to react like a grownup—she saw herself being calm, cool, offering help to whoever might have needed it in the classroom—but the tears and the shaking would not stop.

Mr. Brant had seemed angry, as if the entire classroom were at fault. Not only was Mr. Brant adult, he was PPC.

So did she expect adults, especially adult PPCs, to behave better?

Wasn't that what it was all about?

She stared at herself in the cracked mirror. "I should go home, or go to the library and study," she said. Dignity and decorum. Two girls walked into the lavatory, and her private moment passed.

Letitia did not go to the library. Instead, she went to the old concrete and steel auditorium, entering through the open stage entrance, standing in darkness in the wings. Three female students sat in the front row, below the stage level and about ten meters away from Letitia. She recognized Reena but not the other two; they did not share classes with her.

"Did you know him?"

"No, not very well," Reena said. "He was in my class."

"No ducks!" the third snorted.

"Trish, keep it *interior,* please. Reena's had it rough."

"He hadn't blitzed. He wasn't a superwhiz. Nobody expected it."

"When was his incept?"

"I don't know," Reena said. "We're all about the

same age, within a couple of months. We're all the same model year, same supplements, if it's something in the genotype, in the supplements . . ."

"I heard somebody say there had been five so far. I haven't heard anything," the third said.

"I haven't either," said the second.

"Not in our school," Reena said. "Except for the superwhizes. And none of them have died before now."

Letitia stepped back in the darkness, hand on mouth. Had Lockwood actually died?

She thought for a mad moment of stepping out of the wings, going into the seats and telling the three she was sorry. The impulse faded fast. That would have been intruding.

They weren't any older than she was, and they didn't sound much more mature. They sounded scared.

In the morning, at the station room for pre-med secondary, Brant told them that John Lockwood had died the day before. "He had a heart attack," Brant said. Letitia intuited that was not the complete truth. A short eulogy was read, and special hours for psych counseling were arranged for those students who felt they might need it.

The word "blitzing" was not mentioned by Brant, nor by any of the PPCs throughout that day. Letitia tried to research the subject but found precious few materials in the libraries accessed by her mod. She presumed she didn't know where to look; it was hard to believe that *nobody* knew what was happening.

The dream came again, even stronger, the next night, and Letitia awoke out of it cold and shivering

24

with excitement. She saw herself standing before a crowd, no single face visible, for she was in light and they were in darkness. She had felt, in the dream, an almost unbearable happiness, grief mixed with joy, unlike anything she had ever experienced before. She *loved* and did not know what she loved—not the crowd, precisely, not a man, not a family member, not even herself.

She sat up in her bed, hugging her knees, wondering if anybody else was awake. It seemed possible she had never been awake until now; every nerve was alive. Quietly, not wanting anybody else to intrude on this moment, she slipped out of bed and walked down the hall to her mother's sewing room. There, in a full-length cheval mirror, she looked at herself as if with new eyes.

"Who are you?" she whispered. She lifted her cotton nightshirt and stared at her legs. Short calves, lumpy knees, thighs not bad—not fat, at any rate. Her arms were softlooking, not muscular, but not particularly plump, a rosy vanilla color with strawberry blotches on her elbows where she leaned on them while reading in bed. She had Irish ancestors on her mother's side; that showed in her skin color, recessed cheekbones, broad face. On her father's side, Mexican and German; not much evidence in her of the Mexican. Her brother looked more swarthy. "We're mongrels," she said. "I look like a mongrel compared to PPC purebreds." But PPCs were not purebred; they were *designed*.

She lifted her nightshirt higher still, pulling it over her head finally and standing naked. Shivering from the cold and from the memory of her dream, she forced herself to focus on all of her characteristics. Whenever she had seen herself naked in mirrors before, she had blurred her eyes at one feature, looked away from another, special-effecting her body into a more acceptable fantasy. Now she was in a mood to know herself for what she was.

Broad hips, strong abdomen—plump, but strong. From her pre-med, she knew that meant she would probably have little trouble bearing children. "Brood mare," she said, but there was no critical sharpness in the words. To have children, she would have to attract men, and right now there seemed little chance of that. She did not have the "Attraction Peaks" so often discussed on the TV, or seen faddishly headlined on the LitVid mods; the culturally prescribed geometric curves allocated to so few naturally, and now available to so many by design. *Does Your Child Have the Best Design for Success?*

Such a shocking triviality. She felt a righteous anger grow—another emotion she was not familiar with—and sucked it back into the excitement, not wanting to lose her mood. "I might never look at myself like this again," she whispered.

Her breasts were moderate in size, the left larger than the right and more drooping. She could indeed hold a stylus under her left breast, something a PPC female would not have to worry about for decades, if ever. Rib cage not really distinct; muscles not distinct; rounded, soft, gentle-looking, face curious, friendly, wide-eyed, skin blemished but not so badly it wouldn't recover on its own; feet long and toenails thick, heavily cuticled. She had never suffered from ingrown toenails.

Her family line showed little evidence of tendency to cancer—correctible now, but still distressing—or heart disease or any of the other diseases of melting pot cultures, of mobile populations and changing habits. She saw a strong body in the mirror, one that would serve her well.

And she also saw that with a little makeup, she could easily play an older woman. Some shadow under the eyes, lines to highlight what would in thirty or forty years be jowls, laugh lines ...

But she did not look old *now*.

Letitia walked back to her room, treading carefully on the carpet. In the room, she asked the lights to turn on, lay down on the bed, pulled the photo album Jane had given her from the top of her nightstand and gingerly turned the delicate black paper pages. She stared at her great-grandmother's face, and then at the picture of her grandmother as a little girl.

Individual orchestra was taught by three instructors in one of the older drama classrooms behind the auditorium. It was a popular aesthetic; the school's music boxes were better than most home units, and the instructors were very popular. All were PPCs.

After a half-hour of group, each student could retire to box keyboard, order up spheres of countersound to avoid cacophony, and practice.

Today, she practiced for less than half an hour. Then, tongue between her lips, she stared into empty space over the keyboard. "Countersound off, please," she ordered, and stood up from the black bench. Mr. Teague, the senior instructor, asked if she were done for the day.

"I have to run an errand," she said.

"Practice your polyrhythms," he advised.

She left the classroom and walked around to the auditorium's stage entrance. She knew Reena's drama group would be meeting there.

The auditorium was dark, the stage lighted by a few catwalk spots. The drama group sat in a circle of chairs in one illuminated corner of the stage, reading lines aloud from old paper scripts. Hands folded, she walked toward the group. Rick Fayette, a quiet senior with short black hair, spotted her first but said nothing, glancing at Reena. Reena stopped reading her lines, turned, and stared at Letitia. Edna Corman saw her last and shook her head, as if this were the last straw.

"Hello," Letitia said.

"What are you doing here?" There was more wonder than disdain in Reena's voice.

"I thought you might still . . ." She shook her head.

"Probably not. But I thought you might still be able to use me."

"Really," Edna Corman said.

Reena put her script down and stood. "Why'd you change your mind?"

"I thought I wouldn't mind being an old lady," Reena said. "It's just not that big a deal. I brought a picture of my great-grandmother." She took a plastic wallet from her pocket and opened it to a copy she had made from the photo in the album. "You could make me up like this. Like my great-grandmother."

Reena took the wallet. "You look like her," she said.
"Yeah. Kind of."

"Look at this," Reena said, holding the picture out
to the others. They gathered around and passed the
wallet from hand to hand, staring in wonder. Even
Edna Corman glanced at it briefly. "She actually *looks*
like her great-grandmother."

Rick Fayette whistled with wonder. "You," he said,
"will make a really great old lady."

Rutger called her into his office abruptly a week later.
She sat quietly before his desk. "You've joined the
drama class after all," he said. She nodded.

"Any reason?"

There was no simple way to express it. "Because of
what you told me," she said.

"No friction?"

"It's going okay."

"Very good. They gave you another role to play?"

"No. I'm the old lady. They'll use makeup on me."

"You don't object to that?"

"I don't think so."

Rutger seemed to want to find something wrong,
but he couldn't. With a faintly suspicious smile, he
thanked her for her time. "Come back and see me
whenever you want," he said. "Tell me how it goes."

The group met each Friday, an hour later than her
individual orchestra. Letitia made arrangements for
home keyboard hookup and practice. After a reading
and a half-hour of questions, she obtained the per-
mission of the drama group advisor, a spinsterish
non-PPC seldom seen in the hallways, Miss Darcy.

Miss Darcy seemed old-fashioned and addressed all of her students as either "Mister" or "Miss," but she knew drama and stagecraft. She was the oldest of the six NG teachers in the school.

Reena stayed with Letitia during the audition and made a strong case for her late admittance, saying that the casting of Rick Fayette as an older woman was not going well. Fayette was equally eager to be rid of the part; he had another nonconflicting role, and the thought of playing two characters in this production worried him.

Fayette confessed his appreciation at their second Friday meeting. He introduced her to an elfishly handsome, large-eyed, slender group member, Frank Leroux. Leroux was much too shy to go on stage, Fayette said, but he would be doing their makeup. "He's pretty amazing."

Letitia stood nervously while Leroux examined her. "You've really got a *face*," he said softly. "May I touch you, to see where your contours are?"

Letitia giggled and abruptly sobered, embarrassed. "Okay," she said. "You're going to draw lines and make shadows?"

"Much more than that," Leroux said.

"He'll take a video of your face in motion," Fayette said. "Then he'll digitize it and sculpt a laserfoam mold—much better than sitting for a life mask. He made a life mask of *me* last year to turn me into the Hunchback of Notre Dame. No fun at all."

"This way is much better," Leroux said, touching her skin delicately, poking under her cheeks and chin, pulling back her hair to feel her temples. "I can make two or three sculptures showing what your face and neck are like when they're in different positions. Then I can adjust the appliance molds for flex and give."

"When he's done with you, you won't know yourself," Fayette said.

"Reena says you have a picture of your great-grandmother. May I see it?" Leroux asked. She gave him the wallet and he looked at the picture with squint-eyed intensity. "What a wonderful face," he said. "I never met my great-grandmother. My own grandmother looks about as old as my mother. They might be sisters."

"When he's done with you," Fayette said, his enthusiasm becoming a bit tiresome, "you and your *great-grandmother* will look like sisters!"

When she went home that evening, taking a late pay metro from the school, she wondered just exactly what she was doing. Throughout her high school years, she had cut herself off from most of her fellow students; the closest she came to friendship had been occasional banter while sitting at the mods with John Lockwood, waiting for instructors to arrive. Now she actually liked Fayette, and strange Leroux, whose hands were thin and pale and strong and slightly cold. Leroux was a PPC, but obviously his parents had different tastes; was he a superwhiz? Nobody had said so; perhaps it was a matter of honor among PPCs that they pretended not to care about their classifications.

Reena was friendly and supportive, but still distant. As Letitia walked up the stairs, across the porch into the door of their home, setting her keyboard down by the closet, she saw the edge of a news broadcast in the living room. Nobody was watching; she surmised everybody was in the kitchen.

From this angle, the announcer appeared translucent and blue, ghostly. As Letitia walked around to the premium angle, the announcer solidified, a virtual goddess of Asian-Negroid features with high cheekbones, straight golden hair and copper-bronze skin. Letitia didn't care what she looked like; what she was saying had attracted her attention.

"—revelations made today that as many as one-fourth of all PPCs inceived between sixteen and seventeen years ago may be possessors of a defective chromosome sequence known as T56-WA 5659. Originally part of an intelligence enhancement macrobox used in ramping creativity and mathematical ability, T56-WA 5659 was refined and made a standard option in virtually all pre-planned children. The effects of this defective sequence are not yet known, but at least twenty children in our city have already died. They all suffered from initial symptoms similar to grand mal epilepsy. Nationwide casualties are as yet unknown. The Rifkin Society is charging government regulatory agencies with a wholesale cover-up.

"The Parental Pre-Natal Design Administration has advised parents of PPC children with this incept to immediately contact your medicals and design specialists for advice and treatment. Younger children may be eligible to receive wholebody retroviral therapy. For more detailed information, please refer to our LitVid on-line at this moment, and call—"

Letitia turned and saw her mother watching with a kind of grim satisfaction. When she noticed her daughter's shocked expression, she suddenly appeared sad. "How unfortunate," she said. "I wonder how far it will go."

Letitia did not eat much dinner. Nor did she sleep more than a couple of hours that night. The weekend seemed to stretch on forever.

Leroux compared the laserfoam sculptures to her face, turning her chin this way and that with gentle hands before the green room mirror. As Leroux worked to test the various molds on Letitia, humming softly to himself, the rest of the drama group rehearsed a scene that did not require her presence. When they were done, Reena walked into the green room and stood behind them, watching. Letitia smiled stiffly through the hastily applied sheets and mounds of skinlike plastic.

"You're going to look great," Reena said.

"I'm going to look *old*," Letitia said, trying for a joke.

"I hope you aren't worried about that," Reena said. "Nobody cares, really. They all like you. Even Edna."

"I'm not worried," Letitia said.

Leroux pulled off the pieces and laid them carefully in a box. "Just about got it," he said. "I'm getting so good I could even make *Reena* look old if she'd let me."

Letitia considered for a moment. The implication, rather than the meaning, was embarrassingly obvious. Reena blushed and stared angrily at Leroux. Leroux caught her stare, looked between them, and said, "Well, I could." Reena could not argue without sinking them all deeper. Letitia blinked, then decided to let them off this particular hook. "She wouldn't look like a grandmother, though. I'll be a much better old lady."

"Of course," Leroux said, picking up his box and the sculptures. He walked to the door, a mad headsman. "Like your great-grandmother."

For a long silent moment, Reena and Letitia faced each other alone in the green room. The old incandescent makeup lights glared around the cracked mirror, casting a pearly glow on the white walls behind them. "You're a good actress," Reena said. "It really doesn't matter what you look like."

"Thank you."

"Sometimes I wished I looked like somebody in my family," Reena said.

Without thinking, Letitia said, "But you're beautiful." And she meant it. Reena *was* beautiful; with her Levantine darkness and long black hair, small sharp chin, large hazelcolored almond eyes and thin, everso-slightly bowed nose, she was simply lovely, with the kind of face and bearing and intelligence that two or three generations before would have moved her into entertainment, or pushed her into the social circles of the rich and famous. Behind the physical beauty was a sparkle of reserved wit, and something gentle. PPCs were healthier, felt better, and their minds, on the average, were more subtle, more balanced. Letitia did not feel inferior, however; not this time.

Something magic touched them. The previous awkwardness, and her deft destruction of that awkwardness, had moved them into a period of charmed conversation. Neither could offend the other; without words, that was a given.

"My parents are beautiful, too. I'm second generation," Reena said.

"Why would you want to look any different?"

"I don't, I suppose. I'm happy with the way I look. But I don't look much like my mother or my father. Oh, color, hair, eyes, that sort of thing . . . Still, my mother wasn't happy with her own face. She didn't get along well with my grandmother . . . She blamed her for not matching her face with her personality." Reena smiled. "It's all rather silly."

"Some people are never happy," Letitia observed.

Reena stepped forward and leaned over slightly to face

Letitia's mirror image. "How do you feel, looking like your grandmother?"

Letitia bit her lip. "Until you asked me to join, I don't think I ever knew." she told about her mother giving her the album, and looking at herself in the mirror—though she did not describe being naked—and comparing herself with the old pictures.

"I think that's called an epiphany," Reena said. "It must have been nice. I'm glad I asked you, then, even if I was stupid."

"Were you . . ." Letitia paused. The period of charm was fading, regrettably; she did not know whether this question would be taken as she meant it. "Did you ask me to give me a chance to stop being so silly and stand-offish?"

"No," Reena said steadily. "I asked you because we needed an old lady."

Looking at each other, they laughed suddenly, and the charmed moment was gone, replaced by something steadier and longer-lasting: friendship. Letitia took Reena's hand and pressed it. "Thank you," she said.

"You're welcome." Then, with hardly a pause, Reena said, "At least you don't have to worry."

Letitia stared up at her, mouth open, eyes searching.

"Got to go home now," Reena said. She squeezed Letitia's shoulder with more than gentle strength, revealing a physical anger or jealousy that ran counter to all they had said and done thus far. She turned and walked through the green room door, leaving Letitia alone to pick off a few scraps of latex and adhesive.

The disaster grew. Letitia listened to the news in her room late that night, whispers in her ear, projected ghosts of newscasters and doctors and scientists dancing before her eyes, telling her things she did not really understand, could only feel.

A monster walked through her generation, but it would not touch her.

Going to school on Monday, she saw students clustered in hallways before the bell, somber, talking in low voices, glancing at her as she passed. In her second period class, she learned from overheard conversation that Leroux had died during the weekend. "He was superwhiz," a tall, athletic girl told her neighbor. "They don't die, usually, they just blitz. But he died."

Letitia retreated to the old lavatory at the beginning of lunch break, found it empty, but did not stare into the mirror. She knew what she looked like and accepted it.

What she found difficult to accept was a new feeling inside her. The young Letitia was gone. She could not live on a battlefield and remain a child. She thought about slender, elfin Leroux, carrying her heads under his arms, touching her face with gentle, professional admiration. Strong, cool fingers. Her eyes filled but the tears would not fall, and she went to lunch empty, fearful, confused.

She did not apply for counseling, however. This was something she had to face on her own.

Nothing much happened the next few days. The rehearsals went smoothly in the evenings as the date of the play approached. She learned her lines easily enough. Her role had a sadness that matched her mood. On Wednesday evening, after rehearsal, she joined Reena and Fayette at a supermarket sandwich stand near the school. Letitia did not tell her parents she would be late; she felt the need to not be responsible to anybody but her immediate peers. Jane would be upset, she knew, but not for long; this was a *necessity.*

Neither Reena nor Fayette mentioned the troubles directly. They were fairylike in their gaiety. They kidded Letitia about having to do without makeup now, and it seemed funny, despite their hidden grief. They ate sandwiches and drank fruit sodas and talked about what they would be when they grew up.

"Things didn't used to be so easy," Fayette said. "Kids didn't have so many options. Schools weren't very efficient at training for the real world; they were academic."

"Learning was slower," Letitia said.

"So were the kids," Reena said, tossing off an irresponsible grin.

"I resent that," Letitia said. Then, together, they all said, *"I don't deny it, I just resent it!"* Their laughter caught the attention of an older couple sitting in a corner. Even if the man and woman were not angry, Letitia wanted them to be, and she bowed her head down, giggling into her straw, snucking bubbles up her nose and choking. Reena made a disapproving face and Fayette covered his mouth, snorting with laughter.

"You could paste rubber all over your face," Fayette suggested.

"I'd look like Frankenstein's monster, not an old woman," Letitia said.

"So what's the difference?" Reena said.

"Really, you guys," Letitia said. "You're acting your age."

"Don't have to act," Fayette said. "Just *be.*"

"I wish we could act our age," Reena said.

Not once did they mention Leroux, but it was as if he sat beside them the whole time, sharing their levity.

It was the closest thing to a wake they could have.

"Have you gone to see your designer, your medical?" Letitia asked Reena behind the stage curtains. The lights were off. Student stagehands moved muslin walls on dollies. Fresh paint smells filled the air.

"No," Reena said. "I'm not worried. I have a different incept."

"Really?"

She nodded. "It's okay. If there was any problem, I wouldn't be here. Don't worry." And nothing more was said.

The night of dress rehearsal came. Letitia put on her own makeup, drawing pencil lines and applying color and shadow; she had practiced and found herself reasonably adept at aging. With her great-grandmother's photograph before her, she mimicked the jowls she would have in her later years, drew laugh lines around her lips, and completed the effect with a smelly old gray wig dug out of a prop box.

The actors gathered for a prerehearsal inspection by Miss Darcy. They seemed quite adult now, dressed in their period costumes, tall and handsome. Letitia didn't mind standing out. Being an old woman gave her special status.

"This time, just relax, do it smooth," said Miss Darcy. "Everybody expects you to flub your lines, so you'll probably do them all perfectly. We'll have an audience, but they're here to forgive our mistakes, not laugh at them. This one," Miss Darcy said, pausing, "is for Mr. Leroux."

They all nodded solemnly.

"Tomorrow, when we put on the first show, that's going to be for you."

They took their places in the wings. Letitia stood behind Reena, who would be first on stage. Reena shot her a quick smile, nervous.

"How's your stomach?" she whispered.

"Where's the bag?" Letitia asked, pretending to gag herself with a finger.

"TB," Reena accused lightly

"RC," Letitia replied. They shook hands firmly.

The curtain went up. The auditorium was half filled with parents and friends and relatives. Letitia' s parents were out there. The darkness beyond the stagelights seemed so profound it should have been filled with stars and nebulae. Would her small voice reach that far?

The recorded music before the first act came to its quiet end. Reena made a move to go on stage, then stopped. Letitia nudged her. "Come on."

Reena pivoted to look at her, face cocked to one side, and Letitia saw a large tear dripping from her left eye. Fascinated, she watched the tear fall in slow motion down her cheek and spot the satin of her gown.

"I'm sorry," Reena whispered, lips twitching. "I can't do it now. Tell. Tell."

Horrified, Letitia reached out, tried to stop her from falling, to lift her, paste and push her back into place, but Reena was too heavy and she could not stop her descent, only slow it. Reena's feet kicked out like a horse's, bruising Letitia's legs, all in apparent silence, and her eyes were bright and empty and wet, fluttering, showing the whites.

Letitia bent over her, hands raised, afraid to touch her, afraid not to, unaware she was shrieking.

Fayette and Edna Corman stood behind her, equally helpless.

Reena lay still like a twisted doll, face upturned, eyes moving slowly to Letitia, vibrating, becoming still.

"Not you!" Letitia screamed, and barely heard the commotion in the audience. "Please, God, let it be me, not her!"

Fayette backed away and Miss Darcy came into the light, grabbing Letitia's shoulders. She shook free.

"Not her," Letitia sobbed. The medicals arrived and surrounded Reena, blocking her from the eyes of all around. Miss Darcy firmly, almost brutally, pushed her students from the stage and herded them into the green room. Her face was stiff as a mask, eyes stark in the paleness.

"We have to *do* something!" Letitia said, holding up her hands, beseeching.

"Get control of yourself," Miss Darcy said sharply. "Everything's being done that can be done."

Fayette said, "What about the play?"

Everyone stared at him.

"Sorry," he said, lip quivering. "I'm an idiot."

Jane, Donald, and Roald came to the green room and Letitia hugged her mother fiercely, eyes shut tight, burying her face in Jane's shoulder. They escorted her outside, where a few students and parents still milled about in the early evening. "We should go home," Jane said.

"We have to stay here and find out if she's all right." Letitia pushed away from Jane's arms and looked at the people. "They're so frightened. I know they are. She's frightened, too. 1 saw her. She told me—" Her voice hitched. "She told me—"

"We'll stay for a little while," her father said. He walked off to talk to another man. They conversed for a while, the man shook his head, they parted. Roald stood away from them, hands stuffed into his pockets, dismayed, young, uncomfortable.

"All right," Donald said a few minutes later. "We're not going to find out anything tonight. Let's go home."

This time, she did not protest. Home, she locked herself in her bedroom. She did not need to know. She had seen it happen; anything else was self-delusion.

Her father came to the door an hour later, rapped gently. Letitia came up from a troubled doze and got off the bed to let him in.

"We're very sorry," he said.

"Thanks," she murmured, returning to the bed. He sat beside her. She might have been eight or nine again; she looked around the room, at toys and books, knickknacks.

"Your teacher, Miss Darcy, called. She said to tell you, Reena Cathcart died. She was dead by the time they got her to the hospital. Your mother and I have been watching the vids. A lot of children are very sick now. A lot have died." He touched her head, patted the crown gently. "I think you know now why we wanted a natural child. There were risks."

"That's not fair," she said. "You didn't have us . . ." She hiccupped. "The way you did, because you thought there would be risks. You talk as if there's something wrong with these . . . people."

"Isn't there?" Donald asked, eyes suddenly flinty. "They're defective."

"They're my friends!" Letitia shouted.

"Please," Donald said, flinching.

42

She got to her knees on the bed, tears coming again. "There's nothing wrong with them! They're people! They're just sick, that's all."

"You're not making sense," Donald said.

"I talked to her," Letitia said. "She must have known. You can't just say there's something wrong with them. That isn't enough."

"Their parents should have known," Donald pursued, voice rising. "Letitia . . ."

"Leave me alone," she demanded. He stood up hastily, confused, and walked out, closing the door behind him. She lay back on the bed, wondering what Reena had wanted her to say, and to whom.

"I'll do it," she whispered.

In the morning, breakfast was silent. Roald ate his cereal with caution, glancing at the others with wide, concerned eyes. Letitia ate little, pushed away from the table, said, "I'm going to her funeral."

"We don't know—" Jane said.

"I'm going."

Letitia went to only one funeral: Reena's. With a puzzled expression, she watched Reena's parents from across the grave, wondering about them, comparing them to Jane and Donald. She did not cry. She came home and wrote down the things she had thought.

That school year was the worst. One hundred and twelve students from the school died. Another two hundred became very ill.

John Fayette died.

The drama class continued, but no plays were presented. The school was quiet. Many students had been withdrawn from classes; Letitia watched the hysteria mount, listened to rumors that it was a plague, not a PPC error.

It was not a plague.

Across the nation, two million children became ill. One million died.

Letitia read, without really absorbing the truth all at once, that it was the worst disaster in the history of the United States. Riots destroyed PPC centers. Women carrying PPC babies demanded abortions. The Rifkin Society became a political force of considerable influence.

Each day, after school, listening to the news, everything about her existence seemed trivial. Their family was healthy. They were growing up normally.

Edna Corman approached her in school at the end of one day, two weeks before graduation. "Can we talk?" she asked. "Someplace quiet."

"Sure," Letitia said. They had not become close friends, but she found Edna Corman tolerable. Letitia took her into the old bathroom and they stood surrounded by the echoing white tiles.

"You know, everybody, I mean the older people, they stare at me, at us," Edna said. "Like we're going to fall over any minute. It's really bad. I don't think I'm going to get sick, but . . . It's like people are afraid to touch me."

"I know," Letitia said.

"Why is that?" Edna said, voice trembling.

"I don't know," Letitia said. Edna just stood before her, hands limp.

"Was it our fault?" she asked.

"No. You know that."

"Please tell me."

"Tell you what?"

"What we can do to make it right."

Letitia looked at her for a moment, and then extended her arms, took her by the shoulders, drew her closer, and hugged her. "Remember," she said.

Five days before graduation, Letitia asked Rutger if she could give a speech at the ceremonies. Rutger sat behind his desk, folded his hands, and said, "Why?"

"Because there are some things nobody's saying," Letitia told him. "And they should be said. If nobody else will say them, then . . ." She swallowed hard. "Maybe I can."

He regarded her dubiously for a moment. "You really think there's something important that you can say?"

She faced him down. Nodded.

"Write the speech," he said. "Show it to me."

She pulled a piece of paper out of her pocket. He read it carefully, shook his head—she thought at first in denial—and then handed it back to her.

Waiting in the wings to go on stage, Letitia Blakely listened to the low murmur of the young crowd in the auditorium. She avoided the spot near the curtain.

Rutger acted as master of ceremonies. The proceedings were somber, low-energy. She began to feel as if she were making a terrible mistake. She was too young to say these things; it would sound horribly awkward, even childish.

Rutger made his opening remarks, then introduced

her and motioned for her to come on stage. Letitia deliberately walked through the spot near the curtain, paused briefly, closed her eyes and took a deep breath, as if to infuse herself with whatever remained there of Reena. She walked past Miss Darcy, who seemed to glare at her.

Her throat seized. She rubbed her neck quickly, blinked at the bright lights on the catwalk overhead, tried to see the faces beyond the lights. They were just smudges in great darkness. She glanced out of the corner of her eye and saw Miss Darcy nodding, *Go ahead*.

"This has been a bad time for all of us," she began, voice high and scratchy. She cleared her throat. "I've lost a lot a friends, and so have you. Maybe you've lost sons and daughters. I think, even from there, looking at me, you can tell I'm not ... designed. I'm natural. I don't have to wonder whether I'll get sick and die. But I ..." She cleared her throat again. It wasn't getting easier. "I thought someone like me could tell you something important.

"People have made mistakes, bad mistakes. But you are not the mistakes. I mean ... they weren't mistaken to make you. I can only dream about doing some of the things you'll do. Some of you are made to live in space for a long time, and I can't do that. Some of you will think things I can't, and go places I won't ... travel to see the stars. We're different in a lot of ways, but I just thought it was important to tell you ..." She wasn't following the prepared speech. She couldn't. "I love you. I don't care what the others say. We love you. you are very important. Please don't forget that."

The silence was complete. She felt like slinking away. Instead, she straightened, thanked them, hearing not a word, not a restless whisper, then bowed her head from the catwalk glare and the interstellar darkness beyond.

Miss Darcy, stiff and formal, reached her arm out as Letitia passed by. They shook hands firmly, and Letitia saw, for the first time, that Miss Darcy looked upon her as an equal.

Letitia stood backstage while the ceremonies continued, examining the old wood floor, the curtains, counterweights, and flies, the catwalk.

It seemed very long ago, she had dreamed what she felt now, this unspecified love, not for family, not for herself. Love for something she could not have known back then; love for children not her own, yet hers none the less. Brothers.

Sisters.

Family.

HARDFOUGHT

In the Han Dynasty, historians were appointed by royal edict to write the history of Imperial China. They alone were the arbiters of what would be recorded. Although various emperors tried, none could gain access to the ironbound chest in which each document was placed after it was written. The historians preferred to suffer death rather than betray their trust.

At the end of each reign the box would be opened and the documents published, perhaps to benefit the next emperor. But for these documents, Imperial China, to a large extent, has no history.

The thread survives by whim.

Humans called it the Medusa. Its long twisted ribbons of gas strayed across fifty parsecs, glowing blue, yellow, and carmine. Watery black flecked a central core of ghoulish green. Half a dozen protostars circled the core, and as many more dim conglomerates pooled in dimples in the nebula's magnetic field. The Medusa was a huge womb of stars-—and disputed territory.

Whenever Prufrax looked at the nebula in displays or through the ship's ports, it seemed malevolent, like a zealous mother showing an ominous face to protect her children. Prufrax had never had a mother, but she had seen them in some in the fibs.

At five, Prufrax was old enough to know the *Mellangee's* mission and her role in it. She had already been through four ship-years of indoctrination. Until her first battle she would be educated in both the Know and the Tell. She would be exercised and trained in the Mocks; in sleep she would dream of penetrating the huge red-and-white Senexi seedships and finding the brood mind. "Zap, Zap," she went with her lips, silent so the tellman wouldn't think her thoughts were straying.

The tellman peered at her from his position in the center of the spherical classroom. Her mates stared straight at the center, all focusing somewhere around the tellman's spiderlike teaching desk, waiting for the trouble, some fidgeting. "How many branch individuals in the Senexi brood mind?" he asked. He looked around the classroom. Peered face by face. Focused on her again. "Pru?"

"Five," she said. Her arms ached. She had been pumped full of moans the wake before. She was already three meters tall, in elfstate, with her long, thin limbs not nearly adequately fleshed out and her fingers still crisscrossed with the surgery done to adapt them to the gloves.

"What will you find in the brood mind?" the tell-man pursued, his impassive face stretched across a hammerhead as wide as his shoulders. Some of the fems thought tellmen were attractive. Not many, and Pru was not one of them.

"Yoke," she said.

"What is in the brood-mind yoke?"

"Fibs."

"More specifically? And it really isn't all fib, you know."

"Info. Senexi data."

"What will you do?"

"Zap," she said, smiling.

"Why, Pru?"

"Yoke has team gens-memory. Zap yoke, spill the life of the team's five branch inds."

"Zap the brood, Pru?"

"No," she said solemnly. That was a new instruction, only in effect since her class's inception. "Hold the brood for the supreme overs." The tellman did not say what would be done with the Senexi broods. That was not her concern.

"Fine," said the tellman. "You tell well, for someone who's always half-journeying."

Brainwalk, Prufrax thought to herself. Tellman was fancy with the words, but to Pru, what she was prone to do during Tell was brainwalk, seeking out her future. She was already five, soon six. Old. Some saw Senexi by the time they were four.

"Zap, Zap," she said softly.

* * *

Aryz skidded through the thin layer of liquid ammonia on his broadest pod, considering his new assignment. He knew the Medusa by another name, one that conveyed all the time and effort the Senexi had invested in it. The protostar nebula held few mysteries for him. He and his four branch-mates, who along with the all-important brood mind comprised one of the six teams aboard the seedship, had patrolled the nebula for ninety-three orbits, each orbit—including the timeless periods outside status geometry—taking some one hundred and thirty human years. They had woven in and out of the tendrils of gas, charting the infalling masses and exploring the rocky accretion disks of stars entering the main sequence. With each measure and update, the brood minds refined their view of the nebula, as it would be a hundred generations hence when the Senexi plan would finally mature.

The Senexi were nearly as old as the galaxy. They had achieved spaceflight during the time of the starglobe when the galaxy had been a sphere. They had not been a quick or brilliant race. Each great achievement had taken thousands of generations, and not just because of their material handicaps. In those times elements heavier than helium had been rare, found only around stars that had greedily absorbed huge amounts of primeval hydrogen, burned fierce and blue and exploded early, permeating the ill-defined galactic arms with carbon and nitrogen, lithium and oxygen. Elements heavier than iron had been almost nonexistent. The biologies of cold gas-giant worlds had developed with a much smaller palette of chemical combinations in producing the offspring of the primary Population II stars.

Aryz, even with the limited perspective of a branch ind, was aware that, on the whole, the humans opposing the seedship were more adaptable, more vital. But they were not more experienced. The Senexi with their billions of years had often matched them. And Aryz's perspective was expanding with each day of his new assignment.

In the early generations of the struggle, Senexi mental stasis and cultural inflexibility had made them avoid contact with the Population I species. They had never begun a program of extermination of the younger, newly life-forming worlds; the task would have been monumental and probably useless. So when spacefaring cultures developed, the Senexi had retreated, falling back into the redoubts of old stars even before engaging with the new kinds. They had retreated for three generations, about thirty thousand human years, raising their broods on cold nestworlds around red dwarfs, conserving, holding back for the inevitable conflicts.

As the Senexi had anticipated, the younger Population I races had found need of even the aging groves of the galaxy's first stars. They had moved in savagely, voraciously, with all the strength and mutability of organisms evolved from a richer soup of elements. Biology had, in some ways, evolved in its own right and superseded the Senexi.

Aryz raised the upper globe of his body, with its five silicate eyes arranged in a cross along the forward surface. He had memory of those times, and times long before, though his team hadn't existed then. The brood mind carried memories selected from the total store of nearly twelve billion years' experience; an awesome amount of knowledge, even to a Senexi. He pushed himself forward with his rear pods.

Through the brood mind Aryz could share the memories of a hundred thousand past generations, yet the brood mind itself was younger than its branch individuals. For a time in their youth, in their liquid-dwelling larval form, the branch inds carried their own sacs of data, each a fragment of the total necessary for complete memory. The branch inds swam through ammonia seas and wafted through thick warm gaseous zones, protoplasmic blobs three to four meters in diameter, developing their personalities under the weight of the past—and not even a complete past. No wonder they were inflexible, Aryz thought. Most branch inds were aware enough to see that—especially when they were allowed to compare histories with the Population I species, as he was doing—but there was nothing to be done. They were content the way they were. To change would be unspeakably repugnant. Extinction was preferable ... almost.

But now they were pressed hard. The brood mind had begun a number of experiments. Aryz's team had been selected from the seedship's contingent to oversee the experiments, and Aryz had been chosen as the chief investigator. Two orbits past, they had captured six human embryos in a breeding device, as well as a highly coveted memory storage center. Most Senexi engagements had been with humans for the past three or four generations. Just as the Senexi dominated Population II species, humans were ascendant among their kind.

Experiments with the human embryos had already been conducted. Some had been allowed to develop normally; others had been tampered with, for reasons Aryz was not aware of. The tamperings had not been very successful.

The newer experiments, Aryz suspected, were going to take a different direction, and the seedship's actions now focused on him; he believed he would be given complete authority over the human shapes. Most branch inds would have dissipated under such a burden, but not Aryz. He found the human shapes rather interesting, in their own horrible way. They might, after all, be the key to Senexi survival.

The moans were toughening her elfstate. She lay in pain for a wake, not daring to close her eyes; her mind was changing and she feared sleep would be the end of her. Her nightmares were not easily separated from life; some, in fact, were sharper.

Too often in sleep she found herself in a Senexi trap, struggling uselessly, being pulled in deeper, her hatred wasted against such power . . .

When she came out of the rigor, Prufrax was given leave by the subordinate tellman. She took to the *Mellangee's* greenroads, walking stiffly in the shallow gravity. Her hands itched. Her mind seemed almost empty after the turmoil of the past few wakes. She had never felt so calm and clear. She hated the Senexi double now; once for their innate evil, twice for what they had made her overs put her through to be able to fight them. Logic did not matter. She was calm, assured. She was growing more mature wake by wake. Fight-budding, the tellman called it, hate coming out like blooms, synthesizing the sunlight of his teaching into pure fight.

The greenroads rose temporarily beyond the labyrinth shields and armor of the ship. Simple transparent plastic and steel geodesic surfaces formed a lacework over the gardens, admitting radiation necessary to the vegetation growing along the paths. No machines scooted one forth and inboard here. It was necessary to walk. Walking was luxury and privilege.

Prufrax looked down on the greens to each side of the paths without much comprehension. They were *beautiful*. Yes, one should say that, think that, but what did it mean? Pleasing? She wasn't sure what being pleased meant, outside of thinking Zap. She sniffed a flower that, the signs explained, bloomed only in the light of young stars not yet fusing. They were near such a star now, and the greenroads were shiny black and electric green with the blossoms. Lamps had been set out for other plants unsuited to such darkened conditions. Some technic allowed suns to appear in selected plastic panels when viewed from certain angles. Clever, the technicals.

She much preferred the looks of a technical to a tellman, but she was common in that. Technicals required brainflex, tellmen cargo capacity. Technicals were strong and ran strong machines, like in the adventure fibs, where technicals were often the protags. She wished a technical were on the greenroads with her. The moans had the effect of making her receptive—what she saw, looking in mirrors, was a certain shine in her eyes—but there was no chance of a breeding liaison. She was quite unreproductive in this moment of elfstate. Other kinds of meetings were not unusual.

She looked up and saw a figure at least a hundred meters away, sitting on an allowed patch near the path. She walked casually, gracefully as possible with the stiffness. Not a technical, she saw soon, but she was not disappointed. Too calm.

"Over," he said as she approached.

"Under," she replied. But not by much—he was probably six or seven ship years old and not easily classifiable.

"Such a fine elfstate," he commented. His hair was black. He was shorter than she, but something in his build reminded her of the glovers. She accepted his compliment with a nod and pointed to a spot near him. He motioned for her to sit, and she did so with a whuff, massaging her knees.

"Moans?" he asked.

"Bad stretch," she said.

"You're a glover." He looked at the fading scars on her hands.

"Can't tell what you are," she said.

"Noncombat," he said. "Tuner of the mandates."

She knew very little about the mandates, except that law decreed every ship carry one, and few of the crew were ever allowed to peep. "Noncombat, hm?" she mused. She didn't despise him for that; one never felt strong negatives for a crew member. She didn't feel much of anything. Too calm.

"Been working on ours this wake," he said. "Too hard, I guess. Told to walk." Overzealousness in work was considered an erotic trait aboard the *Mellangee*. Still, she didn't feel too receptive toward him.

"Glovers walk after a rough growing," she said.

He nodded. "My name's Clevo."

"Prufrax."

"Combat soon?"

"Hoping. Waiting forever."

"I know. Just been allowed access to the mandate for a half-dozen wakes. All new to me. Very happy."

"Can you talk about it?" she asked. Information about the ship not accessible in certain rates was excellent barter.

"Not sure," he said, frowning. "I've been told caution."

"Well, I'm listening."

He could come from glover stock, she thought, but probably not from technical. He wasn't very muscular, but he wasn't as tall as a glover, or as thin, either.

"If you'll tell me about gloves."

With a smile she held up her hands and wriggled the short, stumpy fingers. "Sure."

* * *

The brood mind floated weightless in its tank, held in place by buffered carbon rods. Metal was at a premium aboard the Senexi ships, more out of tradition than actual material limitations. From what Aryz could tell, the Senexi used metals sparingly for the same reason—and he strained to recall the small dribbles of information about the human past he had extracted from the memory store—for the same reason that the Romans of old Earth regarded farming as the only truly noble occupation—

Farming being the raising of *plants* for food *and* raw materials. *Plants* were analogous to the freeth Senexi ate in their larval youth, but the freeth were not green and sedentary.

There was always a certain fascination in stretching his mind to encompass human concepts. He had had so little time to delve deeply—and that was good, of course, for he had been set to answer specific questions, not mire himself in the whole range of human filth.

He floated before the brood mind, all these thoughts coursing through his tissues. He had no central nervous system, no truly differentiated organs except those that dealt with the outside world limbs, eyes, permea. The brood mind, however, was all central nervous system, a thinly buffered sac of viscous fluids about ten meters wide.

"Have you investigated the human memory device yet?" the brood mind asked.

"I have."

"Is communication with the human shapes possible for us?"

"We have already created interfaces for dealing with their machines. Yes, it seems likely we can communicate."

"Does it occur to you that in our long war with humans, we have made no attempt to communicate before?"

This was a complicated question. It called for several qualities that Aryz, as a branch ind, wasn't supposed to have. Inquisitiveness, for one. Branch inds did not ask questions. They exhibited initiative only as offshoots of the brood mind.

He found, much to his dismay, that the question had occurred to him. "We have never captured a human memory store before," he said, by way of incomplete answer. 'We could not have communicated without such an extensive source of information."

"Yet, as you say, even in the past we have been able to use human machines."

"The problem is vastly more complex."

The brood mind paused. "Do you think the teams have been prohibited from communicating with humans?"

Aryz felt the closest thing to anguish possible for a branch ind. Was he being considered unworthy? Accused of conduct inappropriate to a branch ind? His loyalty to the brood mind was unshakeable. "Yes."

"And what might our reasons be?"

"Avoidance of pollution."

"Correct. We can no more communicate with them and remain untainted than we can walk on their worlds, breathe their atmosphere." Again, silence.

Aryz lapsed into a mode of inactivity. When the brood mind readdressed him, he was instantly aware.

"Do you know how you are different?" it asked.

"I am not . . ." Again, hesitation. Lying to the brood mind was impossible for him. What snared him was semantics, a complication in the radiated signals between them. He had not been aware that he was different; the brood mind's questions suggested he might be. But he could not possibly face up to the fact and analyze it all in one short time. He signaled his distress.

"You are useful to the team," the brood mind said. Aryz calmed instantly. His thoughts became sluggish, receptive. There was a possibility of redemption. But how was he different? "You are to attempt communication with the shapes yourself. You will not engage in any discourse with your fellows while you are so involved." He was banned. "And after completion of this mission and transfer of certain facts to me, you will dissipate."

Aryz struggled with the complexity of the orders. "How am I different, worthy of such a commission?"

The surface of the brood mind was as still as an undisturbed pool. The indistinct black smudges that marked its radiating organs circulated slowly within the interior, then returned, one above the other, to focus on him. "You will grow a new branch ind. It will not have your flaws, but, then again, it will not be useful to me should such a situation come a second time. Your dissipation will be a relief, but it will be regretted."

"How am I different?"

"I think you know already," the brood mind said. "When the time comes, you will feed the new branch ind all your memories but those of human contact. If you do not survive to that stage of its growth, you will pick your fellow who will perform that function for you."

A small pinkish spot appeared on the back of Aryz's globe. He floated forward and placed his largest permeum against the brood mind's cool surface. The key and command were passed, and his body became capable of reproduction. Then the signal of dismissal was given. He left the chamber.

Flowing through the thin stream of liquid ammonia lining the corridor, he felt ambiguously stimulated. His was a position of privilege and anathema. He had been blessed—and condemned. Had any other branch ind experienced such a thing?

Then he knew the brood mind was correct. He *was* different from his fellows. None of them would have asked such questions. None of them could have survived the suggestion of communicating with human shapes. If this task hadn't been given to him, he would have had to dissipate anyway.

The pink spot grew larger, then began to make grayish flakes. It broke through the skin, and casually, almost without thinking, Aryz scraped it off against a bulkhead. It clung, made a radio-frequency emanation something like a sigh, and began absorbing nutrients from the ammonia.

Aryz went to inspect the shapes.

* * *

She was intrigued by Clevo, but the kind of interest she felt was new to her. She was not particularly receptive. Rather, she felt a mental gnawing as if she were hungry or had been injected with some kind of brain moans. What Clevo told her about the mandates opened up a topic she had never considered before. How did all things come to be—and how did she figure in them?

The mandates were quite small, Clevo explained, each little more than a cubic meter in volume. Within them was the entire history and culture of the human species, as accurate as possible, culled from all existing sources. The mandate in each ship was updated whenever the ship returned to a contact station. It was not likely the *Mellangee* would return to a contact station during their lifetimes, with the crew leading such short lives on the average.

Clevo had been assigned small tasks—checking data and adding ship records—that had allowed him to sample bits of the mandate. "It's mandated that we have records," he explained, "and what we have, you see, is *man-data*." He smiled. "That's a joke," he said. "Sort of."

Prufrax nodded solemnly. "So where do we come from?"

"Earth, of course," Clevo said. "Everyone knows that."

"I mean, where do *we* come from—you and I, the crew."

"Breeding division. Why ask? You know."

"Yes." She frowned, concentrating. "I mean, we

64

don't come from the same place as the Senexi. The same way."

"No, that's foolishness."

She saw that it was foolishness—the Senexi were different all around. What was she struggling to ask? "Is their fib like our own?"

"Fib? History's not a fib. Not most of it, anyway. Fibs are for unreal. History is overfib."

She knew, in a vague way, that fibs were unreal. She didn't like to have their comfort demeaned, though. "Fibs are fun," she said. "They teach Zap."

"I suppose," Clevo said dubiously. "Being noncombat, I don't see Zap fibs."

Fibs without Zap were almost unthinkable to her. "Such dull," she said.

"Well, of course you'd say that. I might find Zap fibs dull—think of that?"

"We're different," she said. "Like Senexi are different."

Clevo's jaw hung open. "No way. We're crew. We're human. Senexi are . . ." He shook his head as if fed bitters.

"No, I mean . . ." She paused, uncertain whether she was entering unallowed territory. "You and I, we're fed different, given different moans. But in a big way we're different from Senexi. They aren't made, nor do they act as you and I. But . . ." Again it was difficult to express. She was irritated. "I don't want to talk to you anymore."

A tellman walked down the path, not familiar to Prufrax. He held out his hand for Clevo, and Clevo grasped it. "It's amazing," the tellman said, "how you two gravitate to each other. Go, elfstate," he addressed Prufrax. "You're on the wrong greenroad."

She never saw the young researcher again. With glover training underway, the itches he aroused soon faded, and Zap resumed its overplace.

The Senexi had ways of knowing humans were near. As information came in about fleets and individual cruisers less than one percent nebula diameter distant, the seedship seemed warmer, less hospitable. Everything was UV with anxiety, and the new branch ind on the wall had to be shielded by a special silicate cup to prevent distortion. The brood mind grew a corniculum automatically, though the toughened outer membrane would be of little help if the seedship were breached.

Aryz had buried his personal confusion under a load of work. He had penetrated the human memory store deeply enough to find instructions on its use. It called itself a *mandate* (the human word came through the interface as a correlated series of radiated symbols), and even the simple preliminary directions were difficult for Aryz. It was like swimming in another family's private sea, though of course infinitely more alien; how could he connect with experiences never had, problems and needs never encountered by his kind?

He could speak some of the human languages in several radio frequencies, but he hadn't yet decided how he was going to produce modulated sound for the human shapes. It was a disturbing prospect. What would he vibrate? A permeum could vibrate subtly—

such signals were used when branch inds joined to form the brood mind but he doubted his control would ever be subtle enough. Sooner expect a human to communicate with a Senexi by controlling the radiations of its nervous system! The humans had distinct organs within their breathing passages that produced the vibrations; perhaps those structures could be mimicked. But he hadn't yet studied the dead shapes in much detail.

He observed the new branch ind once or twice each watch period. Never before had he seen an induced replacement. The normal process was for two brood minds to exchange plasm and form new team buds, then to exchange and nurture the buds. The buds were later cast free to swim as individual larvae. While the larvae often swam through the liquid and gas atmosphere of a Senexi world for thousands, even tens of thousands of kilometers, inevitably they returned to gather with the other buds of their team. Replacements were selected from a separately created pool of "generic" buds only if one or more originals had been destroyed during their wanderings. The destruction of a complete team meant reproductive failure.

In a mature team, only when a branch ind was destroyed did the brood mind induce a replacement. In essence, then, Aryz was already considered dead.

Yet he was still useful. That amused him, if the Senexi emotion could be called amusement. Restricting himself from his fellows was difficult, but he filled the time by immersing himself, through the interface, in the mandate.

The humans were also connected with the mandate

through their surrogate parent, and in this manner they were quiescent.

He reported infrequently to the brood mind. Until he had established communication, there was little to report.

And throughout his turmoil, like the others he could sense a fight was coming. It could determine the success or failure of all their work in the nebula. In the grand scheme, failure here might not be crucial. But the Senexi had taken the long view too often in the past. Their age and experience—their calmness— were working against them. How else to explain the decision to communicate with human shapes? Where would such efforts lead? If he succeeded.

And he knew himself well enough to doubt he would fail.

He could feel an affinity for them already, peering at them through the thick glass wall in their isolated chamber, his skin paling at the thought of their heat, their poisonous chemistry. A diseased affinity. He hated himself for it. And reveled in it. It was what made him particularly useful to the team. If he was defective, and this was the only way he could serve, then so be it.

The other branch inds observed his passings from a distance, making no judgments. Aryz was dead, though he worked and moved. His sacrifice had been fearful. Yet he would not be a hero. His kind could never be emulated.

It was a horrible time, a horrible conflict.

*　*　*

She floated in language, learned it in a trice; there were no distractions. She floated in history and picked up as much as she could, for the source seemed inexhaustible. She tried to distinguish between eyes-open—the barren, pale gray-brown chamber with the thick green wall, beyond which floated a murky roundness—and eyes-shut, when she dropped back into language and history with no fixed foundation.

Eyes-open, she saw the Mam with its comforting limbs and its soft voice, its tubes and extrusions of food and its hissings and removal of waste. Through Mam's wires she learned. Mam also tended another like herself, and another, and one more unlike any of them, more like the shape beyond the green wall.

She was very young, and it was all a mystery.

At least she knew her name. And what she was supposed to do. She took small comfort in that.

They fitted Prufrax with her gloves, and she went into the practice chamber, dragged by her gloves almost, for she hadn't yet knitted her plug-in nerves in the right index digit and her pace control was uncertain.

There, for six wakes straight, she flew with the other glovers back and forth across the dark spaces like elfstate comets. Constellations and nebula aspects flashed at random on the distant walls, and she oriented to them like a night-flying bird. Her glovemates were Ornin, an especially slender male, and Ban, a red-haired female, and the special-projects sisters Ya, Trice, and Damu, new from the breeding division.

When she let the gloves have their way, she was freer than she had ever felt before. Did the gloves really control? The question wasn't important. Control was somewhere uncentered, behind her eyes and beyond her fingers, as if she were drawn on a beautiful silver wire where it was best to go. Doing what was best to do. She barely saw the field that flowed from the grip of the thick, solid gloves or felt its caressing, life-sustaining influence. Truly, she hardly saw or felt anything but situations, targets, opportunities, the success or failure of the Zap. Failure was an acute pain. She was never reprimanded for failure; the reprimand was in her blood, and she felt like she wanted to die. But then the opportunity would improve, the Zap would succeed, and everything around her—stars, Senexi seedship, the *Mellangee,* everything—seemed part of a beautiful dream all her own.

She was intense in the Mocks.

Their initial practice over, the entry play began.

One by one, the special-projects sisters took their hyperbolic formation. Their glove fields threw out extensions, and they combined force. In they went, the mock Senexi seedship brilliant red and white and UV and radio and hateful before them. Their tails swept through the seedship's outer shields and swirled like long silky hair laid on water; they absorbed fantastic energies, grew bright like violent little stars against the seedship outline. They were engaged in the drawing of the shields, and sure as topology, the spirals of force had to have a dimple on the opposite side that would iris wide enough to let in glovers. The sisters twisted the forces, and Prufrax could see the dimple stretching out under them—

The exercise ended. The elfstate glovers were cast into sudden dark. Prufrax came out of the mock unprepared, her mind still bent on the Zap. The lack of orientation drove her as mad as a moth suddenly flipped from night to day. She careened until gently mitted and channeled. She flowed down a tube, the field slowly neutralizing, and came to a halt still gloved, her body jerking and tingling.

"What the breed happened?" she screamed, her hands beginning to hurt.

"Energy conserve," a mechanical voice answered. Behind Prufrax the other elfstate glovers lined up in the catch tube, all but the special-projects sisters. Ya, Trice, and Damu had been taken out of the exercise early and replaced by simulations. There was no way their functions could be mocked. They entered the tube ungloved and helped their comrades adjust to the overness of the real.

As they left the mock chamber, another batch of glovers, even younger and fresher in elfstate, passed them. Ya held up her hands, and they saluted in return. "Breed more every day," Prufrax grumbled. She worried about having so many crew she'd never be able to conduct a satisfactory Zap herself. Where would the honor of being a glover go if everyone was a glover?

She wriggled into her cramped bunk, feeling exhilarated and irritated. She replayed the mocks and added in the missing Zap, then stared gloomily at her small narrow feet.

Out there the Senexi waited. Perhaps they were in the same state as she—ready to fight, testy at being reined in. She pondered her ignorance, her inability to judge whether such feelings were even possible among the enemy. She thought of the researcher, Clevo. "Blank," she murmured. "Blank, blank." Such thoughts were unnecessary, and humanizing Senexi was unworthy of a glover.

Aryz looked at the instrument, stretched a pod into it, and willed. Vocal human language came out the other end, thin and squeaky in the helium atmosphere. The sound disgusted and thrilled him. He removed the instrument from the gelatinous strands of the engineering wall and pushed it into his interior through a stretched permeum. He took a thick draft of ammonia and slid to the human shapes chamber again.

He pushed through the narrow port into the observation room. Adjusting his eyes to the heat and bright light beyond the transparent wall, he saw the round mutated shape first—the result of their unsuccessful experiments. He swung his sphere around and looked at the others.

For a time he couldn't decide which was uglier—the mutated shape or the normals. Then he thought of what it would be like to have humans tamper with Senexi and try to make them into human forms. . . . He looked at the round human and shrunk as if from sudden heat. Aryz had had nothing to do with the experiments. For that, at least, he was grateful.

Apparently, even before fertilization, human buds—eggs—were adapted for specific roles. The healthy human shapes appeared sufficiently different—discounting *sexual* characteristics—to indicate some variation in function. They were four-podded, two-opticked, with auditory apparatus and olfactory organs mounted on the *head*, along with one permeum, the *mouth*. At least, he thought, they were hairless, unlike some of the other Population I species Aryz had learned about in the mandate.

Aryz placed the tip of the vocalizer against a sound-transmitting plate and spoke.

"Zello," came the sound within the chamber. The mutated shape looked up. It lay on the floor, great bloated stomach backed by four almost useless pods. It usually made high-pitched sounds continuously. Now it stopped and listened, straining on the tube that connected it to the breed-supervising device.

"Hello," replied the male. It sat on a ledge across the chamber, having unhooked itself.

The machine that served as surrogate parent and instructor stood in one corner, an awkward parody of a human, with limbs too long and head too small. Aryz could see the unwillingness of the designing engineers to examine human anatomy too closely.

"I am called—" Aryz said, his name emerging as a meaningless stretch of white noise. He would have to do better than that. He compressed and adapted the frequencies. "I am called Aryz."

"Hello," the young female said.

"What are your names?" He knew that well enough, having listened many times to their conversations.

"Prufrax," the female said. "I'm a glover."

The human shapes contained very little genetic

73

memory. As a kind of brood marker, Aryz supposed, they had been equipped with their name, occupation, and the rudiments of environmental knowledge. This seemed to have been artificially imposed; in their natural state, very likely, they were born almost blank. He could not, however, be certain, since human reproductive chemistry was extraordinarily subtle and complicated.

"I'm a teacher, Prufrax," Aryz said. The logic structure of the language continued to be painful to him.

"I don't understand you," the female replied.

"You teach me, I teach you."

"We have the Mam," the male said, pointing to the machine. "She teaches us." The Mam, as they called it, was hooked into the mandate. Withholding that from the humans—the only equivalent, in essence, to the Senexi sac of memory—would have been unthinkable. It was bad enough that humans didn't come naturally equipped with their own share of knowledge.

"Do you know where you are?" Aryz asked.

"Where we live," Prufrax said. "Eyes-open."

Aryz opened a port to show them the stars and a portion of the nebula. "Can you tell where you are by looking out the window?"

"Among the lights," Prufrax said.

Humans, then, did not instinctively know their positions by star patterns as other Population I species did.

"Don't talk to it," the male said. "Mam talks to us." Aryz consulted the mandate for some understanding of the name they had given to the breed-supervising machine. Mam, it explained, was probably a natural expression for womb-carrying parent. Aryz severed the machine's power.

"Mam is no longer functional," he said. He would have the engineering wall put together another less identifiable machine to link them to the mandate and to their nutrition. He wanted them to associate comfort and completeness with nothing but himself.

The machine slumped, and the female shape pulled herself free of the hookup. She started to cry, a reaction quite mysterious to Aryz. His link with the mandate had not been intimate enough to answer questions about the wailing and moisture from the eyes. After a time the male and female lay down and became dormant.

The mutated shape made more soft sounds and tried to approach the transparent wall. It held up its thin arms as if beseeching. The others would have nothing to do with it; now it wished to go with him. Perhaps the biologists had partially succeeded in their attempt at transformation; perhaps it was more Senexi than human.

Aryz quickly backed out through the port, into the cool and security of the corridor beyond.

It was an endless orbital dance, this detection and matching of course, moving away and swinging back, deceiving and revealing, between the *Mellangee* and the Senexi seedship. It was inevitable that the human ship should close in; human ships were faster, knew better the higher geometries.

Filled with her skill and knowledge, Prufrax waited, feeling like a ripe fruit about to fall from the tree. At this point in their training, just before the application, elfstates were very receptive. She was allowed to take a lover, and they were assigned small separate quarters near the outer greenroads.

The contact was satisfactory, as far as it went. Her mate was an older glover named Kumnax, and as they lay back in the cubicle, soothed by air-dance fibs, he told her stories about past battles, special tactics, how to survive.

"Survive?" she asked, puzzled.

"Of course." His long brown face was intent on the view of the greenroads through the cubicle's small window.

"I don't understand," she said.

"Most glovers don't make it," he said patiently.

"I will."

He turned to her. "You're six," he said. "You're very young. I'm ten.

I've seen. You're about to be applied for the first time, you're full of confidence. But most glovers won't make it. They breed thousands of us. We're expendable. We're based on the best glovers of the past, but even the best don't survive."

"I will," Prufrax repeated, her jaw set.

"You always say that," he murmured.

Prufrax stared at him for a moment.

"Last time I knew you," he said, "you kept saying that. And here you are, fresh again."

"What last time?"

"Master Kumnax," a mechanical voice interrupted.

He stood, looking down at her. "We glovers always

have big mouths. They don't like us knowing, but once we know, what can they do about it?"

"You are in violation," the voice said. "Please report to S."

"But now, if you last, you'll know more than the tellman tells."

"I don't understand," Prufrax said slowly, precisely, looking him straight in the eye.

"I've paid my debt," Kumnax said. "We glovers stick. Now I'm going to go get my punishment." He left the cubicle. Prufrax didn't see him again before her first application.

The seedship buried itself in a heating protostar, raising shields against the infalling ice and stone. The nebula had congealed out of a particularly rich cluster of exploded fourth- and fifth-generation stars, thick with planets, the detritus of which now fell on Aryz's ship like hail.

Aryz had never been so isolated. No other branch ind addressed him; he never even saw them now. He made his reports to the brood mind, but even there the reception was warmer and warmer, until he could barely endure to communicate. Consequently—and he realized this was part of the plan—he came closer to his charges, the human shapes. He felt more sympathy for them. He discovered that even between human and Senexi there could be a bridge of need—the need to be useful.

The brood mind was interested in one question: how successfully could they be planted aboard a human ship? Would they be accepted until they could carry out their sabotage, or would they be detected? Already Senexi instructions were being coded into their teachings.

"I think they will be accepted in the confusion of an engagement," Aryz answered. He had long since guessed the general outlines of the brood mind's plans. Communication with the human shapes was for one purpose only; to use them as decoys, insurgents. They were weapons. Knowledge of human activity and behavior was not an end in itself; seeing what was happening to him, Aryz fully understood why the brood mind wanted such study to proceed no further.

He would lose them soon, he thought, and his work would be over. He would be much too human-tainted. He would end, and his replacement would start a new existence, very little different from Aryz—but, he reasoned, adjusted. The replacement would not have Aryz's peculiarity.

He approached his last meeting with the brood mind, preparing himself for his final work, for the ending. In the cold liquid-filled chamber, the great red-and-white sac waited, the center of his team, his existence. He adored it. There was no way he could criticize its action.

Yet—

"We are being sought," the brood mind radiated. "Are the shapes ready?"

"Yes," Aryz said. "The new teaching is firm. They believe they are fully human." And, except for the new teaching, they were. "They defy sometimes." He said nothing about the mutated shape. It would not be used. If they won this encounter, it would probably be placed with Aryz's body in a fusion torch for complete purging.

"Then prepare them," the brood mind said. "They will be delivered to the vector for positioning and transfer."

Darkness and waiting. Prufrax nested in her delivery tube like a freshly chambered round. Through her gloves she caught distant communications murmurs that resembled voices down hollow pipes. The *Mellangee* was coming to full readiness.

Huge as her ship was, Prufrax knew that it would be dwarfed by the seedship. She could recall some hazy details about the seedship's structure, but most of that information was stored securely away from interference by her conscious mind. She wasn't even positive what the tactic would be. In the mocks, that at least had been clear. Now such information either had not been delivered or had waited in inaccessible memory, to be brought forward by the appropriate triggers.

More information would be fed to her just before the launch, but she knew the general procedure. The seedship was deep in a protostar, hiding behind the distortion of geometry and the complete hash of electromagnetic energy. The *Mellangee* would approach, collide if need be. Penetrate. Release. Find. Zap. Her fingers ached. Sometime before the launch she would also be fed her final moans—the tempers—and she would be primed to leave elfstate. She would be a mature glover. She would be a woman.

If she returned
will return
she could become part of the breed, her receptivity
would end in ecstasy rather than mild warmth, she
would contribute second state, naturally born glovers.
For a moment she was content with the thought. That
was a high honor.

Her fingers ached worse.

The tempers came, moans tiding in, then the battle
data. As it passed into her subconscious, she caught a
flash of—

Rocks and ice, a thick cloud of dust and gas glowing red but seeming dark, no stars, no constellation
guides this time. The beacon came on. That would be
her only way to orient once the gloves stopped inertial and locked onto the target.

The seedship
was like
a shadow within a shadow twenty-two kilometers
across, yet carrying only six teams

LAUNCH *She flies!*

Data: the *Mellangee* has buried herself in the seedship, ploughed deep into the interior like a carnivore's
muzzle looking for vitals.

Instruction: a swarm of seeks is dashing through
the seedship, looking for the brood minds, for the
brood chambers, for branch inds. The glovers will
follow.

Prufrax sees herself clearly now. She is the great
avenging comet, bringer of omen and doom, like a
knife moving through the glass and ice and thin, cold
helium as if they weren't there, the chambered round

fired and tearing at hundreds of kilometers an hour through the Senexi vessel, following the seeks.

The seedship cannot withdraw into higher geometries now. It is pinned by the *Mellangee*. It is *hers*.

Information floods *her*, pleases *her* immensely. *She* swoops down orange-and-gray corridors, buffeting against *the* walls like a ricocheting bullet. Almost immediately she comes across a branch ind, sliding through the ammonia film against the outrushing wind, trying to reach an armored cubicle. Her first Zap is too easy, not satisfying, nothing like what she thought. In her wake the branch ind becomes scattered globules of plasma. She plunges deeper.

Aryz delivers his human charges to the vectors that will launch them. They are equipped with simulations of the human weapons, their hands encased in the hideous gray gloves.

The seedship is in deadly peril; the battle has almost been lost at one stroke. The seedship cannot remain whole. It must self-destruct, taking the human ship with it, leaving only a fragment with as many teams as can escape.

The vectors launch the human shapes. Aryz tries to determine which part of the ship will be elected to survive; he must not be there. His job is over, and he must die.

The glovers fan out through the seedship's central hollow, demolishing the great cold drive engines, bypassing the shielded fusion flare and the reprocessing plant, destroying machinery built before their Earth was formed.

The special-projects sisters take the lead. Suddenly

they are confused. They have found a brood mind, but it is not heavily protected. They surround it, prepare for the Zap—

It is sacrificing itself, drawing them in to an easy kill and away from another portion of the seedship. Power is concentrating elsewhere. Sensing that, they kill quickly and move on.

Aryz's brood mind prepares for escape. It begins to wrap itself in flux bind as it moves through the ship toward the frozen fragment. Already three of its five branch inds are dead; it can feel other brood minds dying. Aryz's bud replacement has been killed as well.

Following Aryz's training, the human shapes rush into corridors away from the main action. The special-projects sisters encounter the decoy male, allow it to fly with them . . . until it aims its weapons. One Zap almost takes out Trice. The others fire on the shape immediately. He goes to his death weeping, confused from the very moment of his launch.

The fragment in which the brood mind will take refuge encompasses the chamber where the humans had been nurtured, where the mandate is still stored. All the other brood minds are dead, Aryz realizes; the humans have swept down on them so quickly. What shall he do?

Somewhere, far off, he feels the distressed pulse of another branch ind dying. He probes the remains of the seedship. He is the last. He cannot dissipate now; he must ensure the brood mind's survival.

Prufrax, darting through the crumbling seedship, searching for more opportunities, comes across an injured glover. She calls for a mediseek and pushes on.

The brood mind settles into the fragment. Its support system is damaged; it is entering the time-isolated state, the flux bind, more rapidly than it should. The seals of foamed electric ice cannot quite close off the fragment before Ya, Trice, and Damu slip in. They frantically call for bind-cutters and preservers; they have instructions to capture the last brood mind, if possible.

But a trap falls upon Ya, and snarling fields tear her from her gloves. She is flung down a dark disintegrating shaft, red cracks opening all around as the seedship's integrity fails. She trails silver dust and freezes, hits a barricade, shatters.

The ice seals continue to close. Trice is caught between them and pushes out frantically, blundering into the region of the intensifying flux bind. Her gloves break into hard bits, and she is melded into an ice wall like an insect trapped on the surface of a winter lake.

Damu sees that the brood mind is entering the final phase of flux bind. After that they will not be able to touch it. She begins a desperate Zap
and is too late.

Aryz directs the subsidiary energy of the flux against her. Her Zap deflects from the bind region, she is caught in an interference pattern and vibrates until her tiniest particles stop their knotted whirlpool spins and she simply becomes
space and searing light.

The brood mind, however, has been damaged. It is losing information from one portion of its anatomy.

GREG BEAR

Desperate for storage, it looks for places to hold the information before the flux bind's last wave.

Aryz directs an interface onto the brood mind's surface. The silvery pools of time-binding flicker around them both. The brood mind's damaged sections transfer their data into the last available storage device—the human mandate.

Now it contains both human and Senexi information.

The silvery pools unite, and Aryz backs away. No longer can he sense the brood mind. It is out of reach but not yet safe. He must propel the fragment from the remains of the seedship. Then he must wrap the fragment in its own flux bind, cocoon it in physics to protect it from the last ravages of the humans.

Aryz carefully navigates his way through the few remaining corridors. The helium atmosphere has almost completely dissipated, even there. He strains to remember all the procedures. Soon the seedship will explode, destroying the human ship. By then they must be gone.

Angry red, Prufrax follows his barely sensed form, watching him behind barricades of ice, approaching the moment of a most satisfying Zap. She gives her gloves their way

and finds a shape behind her, wearing gloves that are not gloves, not like her own, but capable of grasping her in tensed fields, blocking the Zap, dragging them together. The fragment separates, heat pours in from the protostar cloud. They are swirled in their vortex of power, twin locked comets—one red, one sullen gray.

"Who are you?" Prufrax screams as they close in on each other in the fields. Their environments meld. They grapple. In the confusion, the darkening, they are drawn out of the cloud with the fragment, and she sees the other's face.

Her own.

The seedship self-destructs. The fragment is propelled from the protostar, above the plane of what will become planets in their orbits, away from the crippled and dying *Mellangee*.

Desperate, Prufrax uses all her strength to drill into the fragment. Helium blows past them, and bits of dead branch inds.

Aryz catches the pair immediately in the shapes chamber, rearranging the fragment's structure to enclose them with the mutant shape and mandate. For the moment he has time enough to concentrate on them. They are dangerous. They are almost equal to each other, but his shape is weakening faster than the true glover. They float, bouncing from wall to wall in the chamber, forcing the mutant to crawl into a corner and howl with fear.

There may be value in saving the one and capturing the other. Involved as they are, the two can be carefully dissected from their fields and induced into a crude kind of sleep before the glover has a chance to free her weapons. He can dispose of the gloves—fake and real—and hook them both to the Mam, reattach the mutant shape as well. Perhaps something can be learned from the failure of the experiment.

The dissection and capture occur faster than the planning. His movement slows under the spreading flux bind. His last action, after attaching the humans to the Mam, is to make sure the brood mind's flux bind is properly nested within that of the ship.

The fragment drops into simpler geometries.

It is as if they never existed.

The battle was over. There were no victors. Aryz became aware of the passage of time, shook away the sluggishness, and crawled through painfully dry corridors to set the environmental equipment going again. Throughout the fragment, machines struggled back to activity.

How many generations? The constellations were unrecognizable. He made star traces and found familiar spectra and types, but advanced in age. There had been a malfunction in the overall flux bind. He couldn't find the nebula where the battle had occurred. In its place were comfortably middle-aged stars surrounded by young planets.

Aryz came down from the makeshift observatory. He slid through the fragment, established the limits of his new home, and found the solid mirror surface of the brood mind's cocoon. It was still locked in flux bind, and he knew of no way to free it. In time the bind would probably wear off—but that might require life spans. The seedship was gone. They had lost the brood chamber, and with it the stock.

He was the last branch ind of his team. Not that it mattered now; there was nothing he could initiate without a brood mind. If the flux bind was permanent—as sometimes happened during malfunction then he might as well be dead.

He closed his thoughts around him and was almost completely submerged when he sensed an alarm from the shapes chamber. The interface with the mandate had turned itself off; the new version of the Mam was malfunctioning. He tried to repair the equipment, but without the engineer's wall he was almost helpless. The best he could do was rig a temporary nutrition supply through the old human-form Mam. When he was done, he looked at the captive and the two shapes, then at the legless, armless Mam that served as their link to the interface and life itself.

She had spent her whole life in a room barely eight by ten meters, and not much taller than her own height. With her had been Grayd and the silent round creature whose name—if it had any—they had never learned. For a time there had been Mam, then another kind of Mam not nearly as satisfactory. She was hardly aware that her entire existence had been miserable, cramped, in one way or another incomplete.

Separated from them by a transparent partition, another round shape had periodically made itself known by voice or gesture.

Grayd had kept her sane. They had engaged in conspiracy. Removing themselves from the interface—what she called "eyes-shut"—they had held on to each other, tried to make sense out of what they knew instinctively, what was fed them through the interface, and what the being beyond the partition told them.

First they knew their names, and they knew that they were glovers. They knew that glovers were fighters. When Aryz passed instruction through the interface on how to fight, they had accepted it eagerly but uneasily. It didn't seem to jibe with instructions locked deep within their instincts.

Five years under such conditions had made her introspective. She expected nothing, sought little beyond experience in the eyes-shut. Eyes-open with Grayd seemed scarcely more than a dream. They usually managed to ignore the peculiar round creature in the chamber with them; it spent nearly all its time hooked to the mandate and the Mam.

Of one thing only was she completely sure. Her name was Prufrax. She said it in eyes-open and eyes-shut, her only certainty.

Not long before the battle, she had been in a condition resembling dreamless sleep, like a robot being given instructions. The part of Prufrax that had taken on personality during eyes-shut and eyes-open for five years had been superseded by the fight instructions Aryz had programmed. She had flown as glovers must fly (though the gloves didn't seem quite right). She had fought, grappling (she thought) with herself, but who could be certain of anything?

She had long since decided that reality was not to be sought too avidly. After the battle she fell back into the mandate—into eyes-shut—all too willingly.

And what matter? If eyes-open was even less comprehensible than eyes-shut, why did she have the nagging feeling eyes-open was so compelling, so necessary? She tried to forget.

But a change had come to eyes-shut, too. Before the battle, the information had been selected. Now she could wander through the mandate at will. She seemed to smell the new information, completely unfamiliar, like a whiff of ocean. She hardly knew where to begin. She stumbled across:

—that all vessels will carry one, no matter what their size or class, just as every individual carries the map of a species. The mandate shall contain all the information of our kind, including accurate and uncensored history, for if we have learned anything, it is that censored and untrue accounts distort the eyes of the leaders. Leaders must have access to the truth. It is their responsibility. Whatever is told those who work under the leaders, for whatever reason, must not be believed by the leaders. Unders are told lies. Leaders must seek and be provided with accounts as accurate as possible, or we will be weakened and fall—

What wonderful dreams the *leaders* must have had. And they possessed some intrinsic gift called *truth*, through the use of the *man-date*. Prufrax could hardly believe that. As she made her tentative explorations through the new fields of eyes-shut, she began to link the word *mandate* with what she experienced. That was where she was.

And she alone. Once, she had explored with Grayd. Now there was no sign of Grayd.

She learned quickly. Soon she walked along a beach on Earth, then a beach on a world called Myriadne, and other beaches, fading in and out. By running through the entries rapidly, she came up with a blurred *eidos* and so learned what a beach was in the abstract. It was a boundary between one kind of eyes-shut and another, between water and land, neither of which had any corollary in eyes-open.

Some beaches had sand. Some had clouds—the *eidos* of clouds was quite attractive. And one—

had herself running scared, screaming.

She called out, but the figure vanished. Prufrax stood on a beach under a greenish-yellow star, on a world called Kyrene, feeling lonelier than ever.

She explored farther, hoping to find Grayd, if not the figure that looked like herself. Grayd wouldn't flee from her. Grayd would. The round thing confronted her, its helpless limbs twitching. Now it was her turn to run, terrified. Never before had she met the round creature in eyes-shut. It was mobile; it had a purpose. Over land, clouds, trees, rocks, wind, air, equations, and an edge of physics she fled. The farther she went, the more distant from the round one with hands and small head, the less afraid she was.

She never found Grayd.

The memory of the battle was fresh and painful. She remembered the ache of her hands, clumsily removed from the gloves. Her environment had collapsed and been replaced by something indistinct. Prufrax had fallen into a deep slumber and had dreamed.

The dreams were totally unfamiliar to her. If there was a left-turning in her arc of sleep, she dreamed of philosophies and languages and other things she couldn't relate to. A right-turning led to histories and sciences so incomprehensible as to be nightmares.

It was a most unpleasant sleep, and she was not at all sorry to find she wasn't really asleep.

The crucial moment came when she discovered how to slow her turnings and the changes of dream subject. She entered a pleasant place of which she had no knowledge but which did not seem threatening. There was a vast expanse of water, but it didn't terrify her. She couldn't even identify it as water until she scooped up a handful. Beyond the water was a floor of shifting particles. Above both was an open expanse, not black but obviously space, drawing her eyes into intense pale blue-green. And there was that figure she had encountered in the seedship. Herself. The figure pursued. She fled.

Right over the boundary into Senexi information. She knew then that what she was seeing couldn't possibly come from within herself. She was receiving data from another source. Perhaps she had been taken captive. It was possible she was now being forcibly debriefed. The tellman had discussed such possibilities, but none of the glovers had been taught how to defend themselves in specific situations. Instead it had been stated—in terms that brooked no second thought that self-destruction was the only answer. So she tried to kill herself.

She sat in the freezing cold of a red-and-white room, her feet meeting but not touching a fluid covering on the floor. The information didn't fit her senses—it seemed blurred, inappropriate. Unlike the other data, this didn't allow participation or motion. Everything was locked solid.

She couldn't find an effective means of killing herself. She resolved to close her eyes and simply will herself into dissolution. But closing her eyes only moved her into a deeper or shallower level of deception—other categories, subjects, visions. She couldn't sleep, wasn't tired, couldn't die.

Like a leaf on a stream, she drifted. Her thoughts untangled, and she imagined herself floating on the water called ocean. She kept her eyes open. It was quite by accident that she encountered:

Instruction. Welcome to the introductory use of the mandate. As a noncombat processor, your duties are to maintain the mandate, provide essential information for your overs, and, if necessary, protect or destroy the mandate. The mandate is your immediate over. If it requires maintenance, you will oblige. Once linked with the mandate, as you are now, you may explore any aspect of the information by requesting delivery. To request delivery, indicate the core of your subject—

Prufrax! she shouted silently. What is Prufrax?

A voice with different tone immediately took over.

Ah, now that's quite a story. I was her biographer, the organizer of her life tapes (ref. GEORGE MACKNAX), and knew her well in the last years of her life. She was born in the Ferment 26468. Here are selected life tapes. Choose emphasis. Analyses follow.

——Hey! Who are you? There's someone here with me. . . .

——Shh! Listen. Look at her. Who is she?

They looked, listened to the information.

--Why, she's *me* . . . sort of.

—She's *us*.

She stood two and a half meters tall. Her hair was black and thick, though cut short; her limbs well-muscled though drawn out by the training and hormonal treatments. She was seventeen years old, one of the few birds born in the solar system, and for the time being she had a chip on her shoulder. Everywhere she went, the birds asked about her mother, Jayax. "You better than her?"

Of course not! Who could be? But she was good; the instructors said so. She was just about through training, and whether she graduated to hawk or remained bird she would do her job well. Asking Prufrax about her mother was likely to make her set her mouth tight and glare.

On Mercior, the Grounds took up four thousand hectares and had its own port. The Grounds was divided into Land, Space, and Thought, and training in each area was mandatory for fledges, those birds embarking on hawk training. Prufrax was fledge three. She had passed Land—though she loathed downbound fighting—and was two years into Space. The tough part, everyone said, was not passing Space, but lasting through four years of Thought after the action in nearorbit and planetary.

Prufrax was not the introspective type. She could be studious when it suited her. She was a quick study at weapon maths, physics came easy when it had a direct application, but theory of service and polin-struc—which she had sampled only in prebird courses—bored her.

Since she had been a little girl, no more than five—

—Five! Five what?

and had seen her mother's ships and fightsuits and fibs, she had known she would never be happy until she had ventured far out and put a seedship in her sights, had convinced a Senexi of the overness of end—

—The Zap! She's talking the Zap!

—What's that?

—You're me, you should know.

—I'm not you, and we're not her.

The Zap, said the mandate, and the data shifted.

"Tomorrow you receive your first implants. These will allow you to coordinate with the zero-angle phase engines and find your targets much more rapidly than you ever could with simple biologic. The implants, of course, will be delivered through your noses—minor irritation and sinus trouble, no more—into your limbic system. Later in your training, hookups and digital adapts will be installed as well. Are there any questions?"

"Yes, sir." Prufrax stood at the top of the spherical classroom, causing the hawk instructor to swivel his platform. "I'm having problems with the zero-angle phase maths. Reduction of the momenta of the real."

Other fledge threes piped up that they, too, had had trouble with those maths. The hawk instructor sighed. "We don't want to install cheaters in all of you. It's bad enough needing implants to supplement biologic. Individual learning is much more desirable. Do you request cheaters?" That was a challenge. They all responded negatively, but Prufrax had a secret smile. She knew the subject. She just took delight in having the maths explained again. She could reinforce an already thorough understanding. Others not so well versed would benefit. She wasn't wasting time. She was in the pleasure of her weapon—the weapon she would be using against the Senexi.

"Zero-angle phase is the temporary reduction of the momenta of the real." Equations and plexes appeared before each student as the instructor went on. "Nested unreals can conflict if a barrier is placed between the participator princip and the assumption of the real. The effectiveness of the participator can be determined by a convenience model we call the angle of phase. Zero-angle phase is achieved by an opaque probability field according to modified Fourier of the separation of real waves. This can also be caused by the reflection of the beam—an effective counter to zero-angle phase, since the beam is always compoundable and the compound is always time-reversed. Here are the true gedanks—"

——Zero-angle phase. She's learning the Zap.

——She hates them a lot, doesn't she?

——The Senexi? They're Senexi.

—I think . . . eyes-open is the world of the Senexi. What does that mean?

—That we're prisoners. You were caught before me.

——Oh.

The news came as she was in recovery from the implant. Seedships had violated human space again, dropping cuckoos on thirty-five worlds. The worlds had been young colonies, and the cuckoos had wiped out all life, then tried to reseed with Senexi forms. The overs had reacted by sterilizing the planet's surfaces. No victory, loss to both sides. It was as if the Senexi were so malevolent they didn't care about success, only about destruction.

She hated them. She could imagine nothing worse.

Prufrax was twenty-three. In a year she would be qualified to hawk on a cruiser/raider. She would demonstrate her hatred.

Aryz felt himself slipping into endthought, the mind set that always preceded a branch ind's self-destruction. What was there for him to do? The fragment had survived, but at what cost, to what purpose? Nothing had been accomplished. The nebula had been lost, or he supposed it had. He would likely never know the actual outcome.

He felt a vague irritation at the lack of a spectrum of responses. Without a purpose, a branch ind was nothing more than excess plasm.

He looked in on the captive and the shapes, all hooked to the mandate, and wondered what he would do with them. How would humans react to the situation he was in? More vigorously, probably. They would fight on. They always had. Even without leaders, with no discernible purpose, even in defeat. What gave them such stamina? Were they superior, more deserving? If they were better, then was it right for the Senexi to oppose their triumph?

Aryz drew himself tall and rigid with confusion. He had studied them too long. They had truly infected him. But here at least was a hint of purpose. A question needed to be answered.

He made preparations. There were signs the brood mind's flux bind was not permanent, was in fact unwinding quite rapidly. When it emerged, Aryz would present it with a judgment, an answer.

He realized, none too clearly, that by Senexi standards he was now a raving lunatic.

He would hook himself into the mandate, improve the somewhat isolating interface he had used previously to search for selected answers. He, the captive, and the shapes would be immersed in human history together. They would be like young suckling on a Population I mother-animal—just the opposite of the Senexi process, where young fed nourishment and information into the brood mind.

The mandate would nourish, or poison. Or both.

—Did she love?
—What—you mean, did she receive?
—No, did she—we—I—give?
—I don't know what you mean.
——I wonder if *she* would know what I mean. . . .
Love, said the mandate, and the data proceeded.
Prufrax was twenty-nine. She had been assigned to a cruiser in a new program where superior but untested fighters were put into thick action with no preliminary. The program was designed to see how well the Grounds prepared fighters; some thought it foolhardy, but Prufrax found it perfectly satisfactory.

The cruiser was a million-ton raider, with a hawk contingent of fifty-three and eighty regular crew. She would be used in a second-wave attack, following the initial hardfought.

She was scared. That was good; fright improved basic biologic, if properly managed. The cruiser would make a raid into Senexi space and retaliate for past cuckoo-seeding programs. They would come up against thornships and seedships, likely.

The fighting was going to be fierce.

The raider made its final denial of the overness of the real and pipsqueezed into an arduous, nasty sponge space. It drew itself together again and emerged far above the galactic plane.

Prufrax sat in the hawks wardroom and looked at the simulated rotating snowball of stars. Red-coded numerals flashed along the borders of known Senexi territory, signifying old stars, dark hulks of stars, the whole ghostly home region where they had first come to power when the terrestrial sun had been a mist-wrapped youngster. A green arrow showed the position of the raider.

She drank sponge-space supplements with the others but felt isolated because of her firstness, her fear. Everyone seemed so calm. Most were fours or fives—on their fourth or fifth battle call. There were ten ones and an upper scatter of experienced hawks with nine to twenty-five battles behind them. There were no thirties. Thirties were rare in combat; the few that survived so many engagements were plucked off active and retired to PR service under the polinstructors. They often ended up in fibs, acting poorly, looking unhappy.

Still, when she had been more naive, Prufrax's heroes had been a man-and-woman thirty team she had watched in fib after fib--Kumnax and Arol. They had been better actors than most.

Day in, day out, they drilled in their fightsuits. While the crew bustled, hawks were put through implant learning, what slang was already calling the Know, as opposed to the Tell, of classroom teaching. Getting background, just enough to tickle her curiosity, not enough to stimulate morbid interest.

--There it is again. Feel?

--I know it. Yes. The round one, part of eyes-open . . .

--Senexi?

--No, brother without name.

--Your . . . brother?

--No . . . I don't know.

--Can it hurt us?

--It never has. It's trying to talk to us.

--*Leave us alone!*

--It's going.

Still, there were items of information she had never received before, items privileged only to the fighters, to assist them in their work. Older hawks talked about the past, when data had been freely available. Stories circulated in the wardroom about the Senexi, and she managed to piece together something of their origins and growth.

Senexi worlds, according to a twenty, had originally been large, cold masses of gas circling bright young suns nearly metal-free. Their gas-giant planets had orbited the suns at hundreds of millions of kilometers and had been dusted by the shrouds of neighboring dead stars; the essential elements carbon, nitrogen, silicon, and fluorine had gathered in sufficient quantities on some of the planets to allow Population II biology.

In cold ammonia seas, lipids had combined in complex chains. A primal kind of life had arisen and flourished. Across millions of years, early Senexi forms had evolved. Compared with evolution on Earth, the process at first had moved quite rapidly. The mechanisms of procreation and evolution had been complex in action, simple in chemistry

There had been no competition between life forms of different genetic bases. On Earth, much time had been spent selecting between the plethora of possible ways to pass on genetic knowledge.

And among the early Senexi, outside of predation there had been no death. Death had come about much later, self-imposed for social reasons. Huge colonies of protoplasmic individuals had gradually resolved into the team-forms now familiar.

Soon information was transferred through the budding of branch inds; cultures quickly developed to protect the integrity of larvae, to allow them to regroup and form a new brood mind. Technologies had been limited to the rare heavy materials available, but the Senexi had expanded for a time with very little technology. They were well adapted to their environment, with few predators and no need to hunt, absorbing stray nutrients from the atmosphere and from layers of liquid ammonia. With perceptions attuned to the radio and microwave frequencies, they had before

long turned groups of branch inds into radio tele-
scope chains, piercing the heavy atmosphere and
probing the universe in great detail, especially the
very active center of the young galaxy. Huge jets of
matter, streaming from other galaxies and emitting
high-energy radiation, had provided laboratories for
their vicarious observations. Physics was a primitive
science to them.

Since little or no knowledge was lost in breeding
cycles, cultural growth was rapid at times; since the
dead weight of knowledge was often heavy, cultural
growth often slowed to a crawl.

Using water as a building material, developing
techniques that humans still understood imperfectly,
they prepared for travel away from their birthworlds.

Prufrax wondered, as she listened to the older
hawks, how humans had come to know all this. Had
Senexi been captured and questioned? Was it all theory? Did anyone really know—anyone she could ask?

—She's weak.

—Why weak?

—Some knowledge is best for glovers to ignore.
Some questions are best left to the supreme overs.

——Have you thought that in here, you can answer
her questions, our questions?

——No. No. Learn about me—us—first.

In the hour before engagement, Prufrax tried to
find a place alone. On the raider this wasn't difficult.
The ship's size was overwhelming for the number of
hawks and crew aboard. There were many areas
where she could put on an environs and walk or drift
in silence, surrounded by the dark shapes of equip-

ment wrapped in plexerv. There was so much about ship operations she didn't understand, hadn't been taught. Why carry so much excess equipment, weapons—far more than they'd need even for replacements? She could think of possibilities—superiors on Mercior wanting their cruisers to have flexible mission capabilities, for one—but her ignorance troubled her less than why she was ignorant. Why was it necessary to keep fighters in the dark on so many subjects?

She pulled herself through the cold g-less tunnels, feeling slightly awked by the loneness, the quiet. One tunnel angled outboard, toward the hull of the cruiser. She hesitated, peering into its length with her environs beacon, when a beep warned her she was near another crewmember. She was startled to think someone else might be as curious as she. The other hawks and crew, for the most part, had long outgrown their need to wander and regarded it as birdish. Prufrax was used to being different—she had always perceived herself, with some pride, as a bit of a freak. She scooted expertly up the tunnel, spreading her arms and tucking her legs as she would in a fightsuit.

The tunnel was filled with a faint milky green mist, absorbing her environs beam. It couldn't be much more than a couple of hundred meters long, however, and it was quite straight. The signal beeped louder.

Ahead she could make out a dismantled weapons blister. That explained the fog: a plexerv aerosol diffused in the low pressure. Sitting in the blister was a man, his environs glowing a pale violet. He had deopaqued a section of the blister and was staring out at the stars. He swiveled as she approached and looked her over dispassionately. He seemed to be a hawk—he had fightform, tall, thin with brown hair above hull-white skin, large eyes with pupils so dark she might have been looking through his head into space beyond.

"Under," she said as their environs met and merged.

"Over. What are you doing here?"

"I was about to ask you the same."

"You should be getting ready for the fight," he admonished.

"I am. I need to be alone for a while."

"Yes." He turned back to the stars. "I used to do that, too."

"You don't fight now?"

He shook his head. "Retired. I'm a researcher."

She tried not to look impressed. Crossing rates was almost impossible. A bitalent was unusual in the service.

"What kind of research?" she asked.

"I'm here to correlate enemy finds."

"Won't find much of anything, after we're done with the zero phase."

It would have been polite for him to say, "Power to that," or offer some other encouragement. He said nothing.

"Why would you want to research them?"

"To fight an enemy properly, you have to know what they are. Ignorance is defeat."

"You research tactics?"

"Not exactly."

"What, then?"

"You'll be in a tough hardfought this wake. Make you a proposition. You fight well, observe, come to me and tell me what you see. Then I'll answer your questions."

"Brief you before my immediate overs?"

"I have the authority," he said. No one had ever lied to her; she didn't even suspect he would. "You're eager?" "Very."

"You'll be doing what?"

"Engaging Senexi fighters, then hunting down branch inds and brood minds."

"How many fighters going in?"

"Twelve."

"Big target, eh?"

She nodded.

"While you're there, ask yourself—what are they fighting for? Understand?"

"I—"

"Ask, what are they fighting for. Just that. Then come back to me." "What's your name?"

"Not important," he said. "Now go."

She returned to the prep center as the sponge-space warning tones began. Overhawks went among the fighters in the lineup, checking gear and giveaway body points for mental orientation. Prufrax submitted to the molded sensor mask being slipped over her face. "Ready!" the overhawk said. "Hard-fought!" He clapped her on the shoulder. "Good luck."

"Thank you, sir." She bent down and slid into her fightsuit. Along the launch line, eleven other hawks did the same. The overs and other crew left the chamber, and twelve red beams delineated the launch tube. The fightsuits automatically lifted and aligned on their individual beams. Fields swirled around them like silvery tissue in moving water, then settled and hardened into cold scintillating walls, pulsing as the launch energy built up.

The tactic came to her. The ship's sensors became part of her information net. She saw the Senexi thornship—twelve kilometers in diameter, cuckoos lacing its outer hull like maggots on red fruit, snakes waiting to take them on.

She was terrified and exultant, so worked up that her body temperature was climbing. The fightsuit adjusted her balance.

At the count of ten and nine, she switched from biologic to cyber. The implant—after absorbing much of her thought processes for weeks—became Prufrax.

For a time there seemed to be two of her. Biologic continued, and in that region she could even relax a bit, as if watching a fib.

With almost dreamlike slowness, in the electronic time of cyber, her fightsuit followed the beam. She saw the stars and oriented herself to the cruiser's beacon, using both for reference, plunging in the sword-flower formation to assault the thornship. The cuckoos retreated in the vast red hull like worms withdrawing into an apple. Then hundreds of tiny black pinpoints appeared in the closest quadrant to the sword flower.

Snakes shot out, each piloted by a Senexi branch

ind. "Hardfought!" she told herself in biologic before
that portion gave over completely to cyber.

> Why were we flung out of dark
> through ice and fire, a shower
> of sparks? a puzzle;
> Perhaps to build hell.

> We strike here, there;
> Set brief glows, fall through
> and cross round again.

> By our dimming, we see what
> Beatitude we have.
> In the circle, kindling
> together, we form an exhausted Empyrean.
> We feel the rush of
> igniting winds but still
> grow dull and wan.

> New rage flames, new light,
> dropping like sun through muddy
> ice and night and fall
> Close, spinning blue and bright.

> In time they, too,
> Tire. Redden.
> We join, compare pasts
> cool in huddled paths, turn gray.

> And again.
> We are a companion flow

of ash, in the slurry,
out and down.
We sleep.

Rivers form above and below.
Above, iron snakes twist,
clang and slice, chime,
helium eyes watching, seeing
Snowflake hawks,
signaling adamant muscles and
energy teeth. What hunger
compels our venom spit?

It flies, strikes the crystal
flight, making mist gray-green
with ammonia rain.

Sleeping, we glide,
and to each side
unseen shores wait
with the moans of
an unseen tide.

—She wrote that. We. One of her-—our—poems."
  —Poem?
  —A kind of fib, I think.
  —I don't see what it says.
  —Sure you do! She's talking hardfought.
  -—The Zap? Is that all?
  —No, I don't think so.
  -—Do you understand it?
  -—Not all . . .

She lay back in the bunk, legs crossed, eyes closed, feeling the receding dominance of the implant—the overness of cyber—and the almost pleasant ache in her back. She had survived her first. The thornship had retired, severely damaged, its surface seared and scored so heavily it would never release cuckoos again.

It would become a hulk, a decoy. Out of action. *Satisfaction/out of action/Satisfaction . . .*

Still, with eight of the twelve fighters lost, she didn't quite feel the exuberance of the rhyme. The snakes had fought very well. Bravely, she might say. They lured, sacrificed, cooperated, demonstrating teamwork as fine as that in her own group. Strategy was what made the cruiser's raid successful. A superior approach, an excellent tactic. And perhaps even surprise, though the final analysis hadn't been posted yet.

Without those advantages, they might have all died.

She opened her eyes and stared at the pattern of blinking lights in the ceiling panel, lights with their secret codes that repeated every second, so that whenever she looked at them, the implant deep inside was debriefed, reinstructed. Only when she fought would she know what she was now seeing.

She returned to the tunnel as quickly as she was able. She floated up toward the blister and found him there, surrounded by packs of information from the last hardfought. She waited until he turned his attention to her.

"Well?" he said.

"I asked myself what they are fighting for. And I'm very angry."

"Why?"

"Because I don't know. I *can't* know. They're Senexi."

"Did they fight well?"

"We lost eight. Eight." She cleared her throat.

"Did they fight well?" he repeated, an edge in his voice.

"Better than I was ever told they could."

"Did they die?"

"Enough of them."

"How many did you kill?"

"I don't know." But she did. Eight.

"You killed eight," he said, pointing to the packs. "I'm analyzing the battle now."

"You're behind what we read, what gets posted?" she asked.

"Partly," he said. "You're a good hawk."

"I knew I would be," she said, her tone quiet, simple.

"Since they fought bravely—"

"How can Senexi be brave?" she asked sharply.

"Since," he repeated, "they fought bravely, why?"

"They want to live, to do their . . . work. Just like me."

"No," he said. She was confused, moving between extremes in her mind, first resisting, then giving in too much. "They're Senexi. They're not like us."

"What's your name?" she asked, dodging the issue.

"Clevo."

Her glory hadn't even begun yet, and already she was well into her fall.

* * *

Aryz made his connection and felt the brood mind's emergency cache of knowledge in the mandate grow up around him like ice crystals on glass. He stood in a static scene. The transition from living memory to human machine memory had resulted in either a coding of data or a reduction of detail; either way, the memory was cold not dynamic. It would have to be compared, recorrelated, if that would ever be possible.

How much human data had had to be dumped to make space for this?

He cautiously advanced into the human memory, calling up topics almost at random. In the short time he had been away, so much of what he had learned seemed to have faded or become scrambled. Branch inds were supposed to have permanent memory, human data, for one reason or another, didn't take. It required so much effort just to begin to understand the different modes of thought.

He backed away from sociological data, trying to remain within physics and mathematics. There he could make conversions to fit his understanding without too much strain.

Then something unexpected happened. He felt the brush of another mind, a gentle inquiry from a source made even stranger by the hint of familiarity. It made what passed for a Senexi greeting, but not in the proper form, using what one branch ind of a team would radiate to a fellow; a gross breach, since it was obviously not from his team or even from his family. Aryz tried to withdraw. How was it possible for minds to meet in the mandate? As he retreated, he pushed into a broad region of incomprehensible data. It had none of the characteristics of the other human regions he had examined.

—This is for machines, the other said. —Not all cultural data is limited to biologic. You are in the area where programs and cyber designs are stored. They are really accessible only to a machine hooked into the mandate.

—What is your family? Aryz asked, the first step-question in the sequence Senexi used for urgent identity requests.

—I have no family. I am not a branch ind. No access to active brood minds. I have learned from the mandate.

—Then what are you?

—I don't know, exactly. Not unlike you.

Aryz understood what he was dealing with. It was the mind of the mutated shape, the one that had remained in the chamber, beseeching when he approached the transparent barrier.

—I must go now, the shape said. Aryz was alone again in the incomprehensible jumble. He moved slowly, carefully, into the Senexi sector, calling up subjects familiar to him. If he could encounter one shape, doubtless he could encounter the others—perhaps even the captive.

The idea was dreadful—and fascinating. So far as he knew, such intimacy between Senexi and human had never happened before. Yet there was something very Senexi-like in the method, as if branch inds attached to the brood mind were to brush mentalities while searching in the ageless memories.

The dread subsided. There was little worse that could happen to him, with his fellows dead, his brood mind in flux bind, his purpose uncertain.

What Aryz was feeling, for the first time, was a small measure of *freedom*.

The story of the original Prufrax continued.

In the early stages she visited Clevo with a barely concealed anger. His method was aggravating, his goals never precisely spelled out. What did he want with her, if anything?

And she with him? Their meetings were clandestine, though not precisely forbidden. She was a hawk one now with considerable personal liberty between exercises and engagements. There were no monitors in the closed-off reaches of the cruiser, and they could do whatever they wished. The two met in areas close to the ship's hull, usually in weapons blisters that could be opened to reveal the stars there they talked.

Prufrax was not accustomed to prolonged conversation. Hawks were not raised to be voluble, nor were they selected for their curiosity. Yet the exhawk Clevo talked a great deal and was the most curious person she had met, herself included, and she regarded herself as uncharacteristically curious.

Often he was infuriating, especially when he played the "leading game," as she called it. Leading her from one question to the next, like an instructor, but without the trappings or any clarity of purpose. "What do you think of your mother?"

"Does that matter?"

"Not to me."

"Then why ask?"

"Because you matter."

Prufrax shrugged. "She was a fine mother. She bore me with a well-chosen heritage. She raised me as a hawk candidate. She told me her stories."

"Any hawk I know would envy you for listening at Jayax's knee."

"I was hardly at her knee."

"A speech tactic."

"Yes, well, she was important to me."

"She was a preferred single?"

"Yes."

"So you have no father."

"She selected without reference to individuals."

"Then you are really not that much different from a Senexi."

She bristled and started to push away. "There! You insult me again."

"Not at all. I've been asking one question all this time, and you haven't even heard. How well do you know the enemy?"

"Well enough to destroy them." She couldn't believe that was the only question he'd been asking. His speech tactics were very odd.

"Yes, to win battles, perhaps. But who will win the war?"

"It'll be a long war," she said softly, floating a few meters from him. He rotated in the blister, blocking out a blurred string of stars. The cruiser was preparing to shift out of status geometry again. "They fight well."

"They fight with conviction. Do you believe them to be evil?"

"They destroy us."

"We destroy them."

"So the question," she said, smiling at her cleverness, "is who began to destroy?"

"Not at all," Clevo said. "I suspect there's no longer a clear answer to that. Our leaders have obviously decided the question isn't important. No. We are the new, they are the old. The old must be superseded. It's a conflict born in the essential difference between Senexi and humans."

"That's the only way we're different? They're old, we're not so old? I don't understand."

"Nor do I, entirely."

"Well, finally!"'

"The Senexi," Clevo continued, unperturbed, "long ago needed only gas-giant planets like their home-worlds. They lived in peace for billions of years before our world was formed. But as they moved from star to star, they learned uses for other types of worlds. We were most interested in rocky Earth-like planets. Gradually we found uses for gas giants, too. By the time we met, both of us encroached on the other's territory. Their technology is so improbable, so unlike ours, that when we first encountered them we thought they must come from another geometry."

"Where did you learn all this?" Prufrax squinted at him suspiciously.

"I'm no longer a hawk," he said, "but I was too valuable just to discard. My experience was too broad, my abilities too useful. So I was placed in research. It seems a safe place for me. Little contact with my comrades." He looked directly at her. "We must try to know our enemy, at least a little."

"That's dangerous," Prufrax said, almost instinctively.

"Yes, it is. What you know, you cannot hate."

"We must hate," she said. "It makes us strong. Senexi hate."

"They might," he said. "But, sometime, wouldn't you like to . . . sit down and talk with one, after a battle? Talk with a fighter? Learn its tactic, how it bested you in one move, compare—"

"No!" Prufrax shoved off rapidly down the tube. "We're shifting now. We have to get ready."

—She's smart. She's leaving him. He's crazy.

—Why do you think that?

—He would stop the fight, end the Zap.

—But he was a hawk.

—And hawks became glovers, I guess. But glovers go wrong, too.

—?

—Did you know they used you? How you were used?

—That's all blurred now.

—She's doomed if she stays around him. Who's that?

—Someone is listening with us.

—Recognize?

—No, gone now.

The next battle was bad enough to fall into the hellfought. Prufrax was in her fightsuit, legs drawn up as if about to kick off. The cruiser exited sponge space and plunged into combat before sponge-space supplements could reach full effectiveness. She was dizzy, disoriented. The overhawks could only hope that a switch from biologic to cyber would cure the problem.

She didn't know what they were attacking. Tactic was flooding the implant, but she was only receiving the wash of that; she hadn't merged yet. She sensed that things were confused. That bothered her. Overs did not feel confusion.

The cruiser was taking damage. She could sense at least that, and she wanted to scream in frustration. Then she was ordered to merge with the implant. Biologic became cyber. She was in the Know.

The cruiser had reintegrated above a gas-giant planet. They were seventy-nine thousand kilometers from the upper atmosphere. The damage had come from ice mines—chunks of Senexi-treated water ice, altered to stay in sponge space until a human vessel integrated nearby. Then they emerged, packed with momentum and all the residual instability of an unsuccessful exit into status geometry. Unsuccessful for a ship, that is—very successful for a weapon.

The ice mines had given up the overness of the real within range of the cruiser and had blasted out whole sections of the hull. The launch lanes had not been damaged. The fighters lined up on their beams and were peppered out into space, spreading in the classic sword flower.

The planet was a cold nest. Over didn't know what the atmosphere contained, but Senexi activity had been high in the star system, concentrating on this world. Over had decided to take a chance. Fighters headed for the atmosphere. The cruiser began planting singularity eggs. The eggs went ahead of the fighters, great black grainy ovoids that seemed to leave a trail of shadow—the wake of a birthing disruption in status geometry that could turn a gas giant into a short-lived sun.

Their time was limited. The fighters would group on entry sleds and descend to the liquid water regions where Senexi commonly kept their upwelling power plants. The fighters would first destroy any plants, loop into the liquid ammonia regions to search for hidden cuckoos, then see what was so important about the world.

She and five other fighters mounted the sled. Growing closer, the hazy clear regions of the atmosphere sparkled with Senexi sensors. Spiderweb beams shot from the six sleds to down the sensors. Buffet began. Scream, heat, then a second flower from the sled at a depth of two hundred kilometers. The sled slowed and held station. It would be their only way back. The fightsuits couldn't pull out of such a large gravity well.

She descended deeper. The pale, bloated beacon of the red star was dropping below the second cloudtops, limning the strata in orange and purple. At the liquid ammonia level she was instructed to key in permanent memory of all she was seeing. She wasn't "seeing" much, but other sensors were recording a great deal, all of it duly processed in her implant. "There's life here," she told herself. Indigenous life. Just another example of Senexi disregard for basic decency:

they were interfering with a world developing its own complex biology.

The temperature rose to ammonia vapor levels, then to liquid water. The pressure on the fightsuit was enormous, and she was draining her stores much more rapidly than expected. At this level the atmosphere was particularly thick with organics.

Senexi snakes rose from below, passed them in altitude, then doubled back to engage. Prufrax was designated the deep diver; the others from her sled would stay at this level in her defense. As she fell, another sled group moved in behind her to double the cover.

She searched for the characteristic radiation curve of an upwelling plant. At the lower boundary of the liquid water level, below which her suit could not safely descend, she found it.

The Senexi were tapping the gas giant's convection from greater depths than usual. Ten kilometers above the plant, almost undetectable, hung another object with an uncharacteristic curve. The power plant was feeding its higher companion with tight energy beams.

She slowed. Two other fighters, disengaged from the brief skirmish above, took backup positions a few dozen kilometers higher. Her implant searched for an appropriate tactic. She would avoid the zero-angle phase for the moment, go in for reconnaissance. She could feel sound pouring from the plant and its companion—rhythmic, not waste noise, but deliberate. And homing in on that sound were waves of large vermiform organisms, like chains of gas-filled sausage. They were dozens of meters long, two meters at their greatest thickness, shaped vaguely like the Senexi snake fighters. The vermiforms were native, and they were being lured into the uppermost floating structure. None were emerging. Her backups spread apart, descended, and drew up along her flanks.

She made her decision almost immediately. She could see a pattern in the approach of the natives. If she fell into the pattern, she might be able to enter the structure unnoticed.

—It's a grinder. She doesn't recognize it.

—What's a grinder?

—She should make the Zap! It's an ugly thing; Senexi use them all the time. Net a planet with grinders, like a cuckoo, but for larger operations.

The creatures were being passed through separator fields. Their organics fell from the bottom of the construct, raw material for new growth—Senexi growth. Their heavier elements were stored for later harvest.

With Prufrax in their midst, the vermiforms flew into the separator. The interior was hundreds of meters wide, lead-white walls with flat gray machinery floating in a dust haze, full of hollow noise, the distant bleats of vermiforms being slaughtered. Prufrax tried to retreat, but she was caught in a selector field. Her suit bucked and she was whirled violently, then thrown into a repository for examination. She had been screened from the separator; her plan to record, then destroy, the structure had been foiled by an automatic filter.

"Information sufficient." Command logic programmed into the implant before launch was now taking over. "Zero-angle phase both plant and adjunct." She was drifting in the repository, still slightly stunned. Something was fading. Cyber was hissing in and out; the over logic-commands were being scrambled. Her implant was malfunctioning and was returning control to biologic. The selector fields had played havoc with all cyber functions, down to the processors in her weapons.

Cautiously she examined the down systems one by one, determining what she could and could not do. This took as much as thirty seconds—an astronomical time on the implant's scale.

She still could use the phase weapon. If she was judicious and didn't waste her power, she could cut her way out of the repository, maneuver and work with her escorts to destroy both the plant and the separator. By the time they returned to the sleds, her implant might have rerouted itself and made sufficient repairs to handle defense. She had no way of knowing what was waiting for her if—when—she escaped, but that was the least of her concerns for the moment.

She tightened the setting of the phase beam and swung her fightsuit around, knocking a cluster of junk ice and silty phosphorescent dust. She activated the beam. When she had a hole large enough to pass through, she edged the suit forward, beamed through more walls and obstacles, and kicked herself out of the repository into free fall. She swiveled and laid down a pattern of wide-angle beams, at the same time relaying a message on her situation to the escorts.

The escorts were not in sight. The separator was beginning to break up, spraying debris through the almost-opaque atmosphere. The rhythmic sound ceased, and the crowds of vermiforms began to disperse.

She stopped her fall and thrust herself several kilometers higher—directly into a formation of Senexi snakes. She had barely enough power to reach the sled, much less fight and turn her beams on the upwelling plant.

Her cyber was still down.

The sled signal was weak. She had no time to calculate its direction from the inertial guidance cyber. Besides, all cyber was unreliable after passing through the separator.

Why do they fight so well? Clevo's question clogged her thoughts. Cursing, she tried to blank and keep all her faculties available for running the fightsuit. *When evenly matched, you cannot win against your enemy unless you understand them. And if you truly understand, why are you fighting and not talking?* Clevo had never told her that—not in so many words. But it was part of a string of logic all her own.

Be more than an automaton with a narrow range of choices. Never underestimate the enemy. Those were old Grounds dicta, not entirely lost in the new training, but only emphasized by Clevo.

If they fight as well as you, perhaps in some ways they fight—think like you do. Use that.

Isolated, with her power draining rapidly, she had no choice. They might disregard her if she posed no danger. She cut her thrust and went into a diving spin. Clearly she was on her way to a high-pressure grave. They would sense her power levels, perhaps even pick up the lack of field activity if she let her shields drop. She dropped the shields. If they let her fall and didn't try to complete the kill—if they concentrated on active fighters above—she had enough power to drop into the water vapor regions, far below the plant, and silently ride a thermal into range. With luck, she could get close enough to lay a web of zero-angle phase and take out the plant.

She had minutes in which to agonize over her plan. Falling, buffeted by winds that could knock her kilometers out of range, she spun like a vagrant flake of snow.

She couldn't even expend the energy to learn if they were scanning her, checking out her potential.

Perhaps she underestimated them. Perhaps they would be that much more thorough and take her out just to be sure. Perhaps they had unwritten rules of conduct like the ones she was using, taking hunches into account. Hunches were discouraged in Grounds training—much less reliable than cyber.

She fell. Temperature increased. Pressure on her suit began to constrict her air supply. She used fighter trancing to cut back on her breathing.

Fell.

And broke the trance. Pushed through the dense smoke of exhaustion. Planned the beam web. Counted her reserves. Nudged into an updraft beneath the plant. The thermal carried her, a silent piece of paper in a storm, drifting back and forth beneath the objective. The huge field intakes pulsed above, lightning outlining their invisible extension. She held back on the beam.

Nearly faded out. Her suit interior was almost unbearably hot.

She was only vaguely aware of laying down the pattern. The beams vanished in the murk. The thermal pushed her through a layer of haze, and she saw the plant, riding high above clear-atmosphere turbulence. The zero-angle phase had pushed through the field intakes, into their source nodes and the plant body, surrounding it with bright blue Cherenkov. First the surface began to break up, then the middle layers, and finally key supports. Chunks vibrated away with the internal fury of their molecular, then atomic, then particle disruption. Paraphrasing Grounds description of beam action, the plant became less and less convinced of its reality. "Matter dreams," an instructor had said a decade before. "Dreams it is real, maintains the dream by shifting rules with constant results. Disturb the dreams, the shifting of the rules results in inconstant results. Things cannot hold."

She slid away from the updraft, found another, wondered idly how far she would be lifted. Curiosity at the last. Let's just see, she told herself; a final experiment.

Now she was cold. The implant was flickering, showing signs of reorganization. She didn't use it. No sense expanding the amount of time until death. No sense—

at all.

The sled, maneuvered by one remaining fighter, glided up beneath her almost unnoticed.

Aryz waited in the stillness of a Senexi memory, his thinking temporarily reduced to a faint susurrus. What he waited for was not clear.

—Come.

The form of address was wrong, but he recognized the voice. His thoughts stirred, and he followed the nebulous presence out of Senexi territory.

—Know your enemy.

Prufrax . . . the name of one of the human shapes sent out against their own kind. He could sense her presence in the mandate, locked into a memory store. He touched on the store and caught the essentials—the grinder, the updraft plant, the fight from Prufrax's viewpoint.

—Know how your enemy knows you.

He sensed a second presence, similar to that of Prufrax. It took him some time to realize that the human captive was another form of the shape, a reproduction of the . . .

Both were reproductions of the female whose image was in the memory store. Aryz was not impressed by threes—Senexi mysticism, what had ever existed of it, had been preoccupied with fives and sixes—but the coincidence was striking.

—Know how your enemy *sees you*.

He saw the grinder processing organics—the vermiform natives—in preparation for a widespread seeding of deuterium gatherers. The operation had evidently been conducted for some time; the vermiform populations were greatly reduced from their usual numbers. Vermiforms were a common type-species on gas giants of the sort depicted. The mutated shape nudged him into a particular channel of the memory, that which carried the original Prufrax's emotions. She had reacted with *disgust* to the Senexi procedure. It was a reaction not unlike what Aryz might feel when coming across something forbidden in Senexi behavior. Yet eradication was perfectly natural, analogous to the human cleansing of *food* before *eating*.

—It's in the memory. The vermiforms are intelligent. They have their own kind of civilization. Human action on this world prevented their complete extinction by the Senexi.

—So what matter they were *intelligent?* Aryz responded. They did not behave or think like Senexi, or like any species Senexi find compatible. They were therefore not desirable. Like humans.

—You would make humans extinct?

—We would protect ourselves from them.

—Who damages whom most?

Aryz didn't respond. The line of questioning was incomprehensible. Instead he flowed into the memory of Prufrax, propelled by another aspect of complete freedom, confusion.

The implant was replaced. Prufrax's damaged limbs and skin were repaired or regenerated quickly, and within four wakes, under intense treatment usually reserved only for overs, she regained all her reflexes and speed. She requested liberty of the cruiser while it returned for repairs. Her request was granted.

She first sought Clevo in the designated research area. He wasn't there, but a message was, passed on to her by a smiling young crew member. She read it quickly:

"You're free and out of action. Study for a while, then come find me. The old place hasn't been damaged. It's less private, but still good. Study! I've marked highlights."

She frowned at the message, then handed it to the crew member, who duly erased it and returned to his duties. She wanted to talk with Clevo, not study.

But she followed his instructions. She searched out highlighted entries in the ship's memory store. It was not nearly as dull as she had expected. In fact, by following the highlights, she felt she was learning more about Clevo and about the questions he asked.

Old literature was not nearly as graphic as fibs, but it was different enough to involve her for a time. She tried to create imitations of what she read, but erased them. Nonfib stories were harder than she suspected. She read about punishment, duty; she read about places called heaven and hell, from a writer who had died tens of thousands of years before. With ed supplement guidance, she was able to comprehend most of what she read. Plugging the store into her implant, she was able to absorb hundreds of volumes in an hour.

Some of the stores were losing definition. They hadn't been used in decades, perhaps centuries.

Halfway through, she grew impatient. She left the research area. Operating on another hunch, she didn't go to the blister as directed, but straight to memory central, two decks inboard the research area. She saw Clevo there, plugged into a data pillar, deep in some aspect of ship history. He noticed her approach, unplugged, and swiveled on his chair. "Congratulations," he said, smiling at her.

"Hardfought," she acknowledged, smiling.

"Better than that, perhaps," he said.

She looked at him quizzically. "What do you mean, better?"

"I've been doing some illicit tapping on over channels."

"So?"

—He *is dangerous!*

"*You've* been recommended."

"For what?"

"Not for hero status, not yet. You'll have a good many more fights before that. And you probably won't enjoy it when you get there. You won't be a fighter then."

Prufrax stood silently before him.

"You may have a valuable genetic assortment. Overs think you behaved remarkably well under impossible conditions."

"Did I?"

He nodded. "Your type may be preserved."

"Which means?"

"There's a program being planned. They want to take the best fighters and reproduce them—clone them—to make uniform top-grade squadrons. It was rumored in my time—you haven't heard?"

She shook her head.

"It's not new. It's been done, off and on, for tens of thousands of years. This time they believe they can make it work."

"You were a fighter, once," she said. "Did they preserve your type?"

Clevo nodded. "I had something that interested them, but not, I think, as a fighter."

Prufrax looked down at her stubby-fingered hands. "It was grim," she said. "You know what we found?"

"An extermination plant."

"You want me to understand them better. Well, I can't. I refuse. How could they do such things?" She looked disgusted and answered her own question. "Because they're Senexi."

"Humans," Clevo said, "have done much the same, sometimes worse."

"No!"

—No!

"Yes," he said firmly. He sighed. "We've wiped Senexi worlds, and we've even wiped worlds with intelligent species like our own. Nobody is innocent. Not in this universe."

"We were never taught that."

"It wouldn't have made you a better hawk. But it might make a better human of you, to know. Greater depth of character. Do you want to be more aware?"

"You mean, study more?"

He nodded.

"What makes you think you can teach me?"

"Because you thought about what I asked you. About how Senexi thought. And you survived where some other hawk might not have. The overs think it's in your genes. It might be. But it's also in your head."

"Why not tell the overs?"

"I have," he said. He shrugged. "I'm too valuable to them, otherwise I'd have been busted again, a long time ago."

"They wouldn't want me to learn from you?"

"I don't know," Clevo said. "I suppose they're aware you're talking to me. They could stop it if they wanted. They may be smarter than I give them credit for." He shrugged again. "Of course they're smart. We just disagree at times."

"And if I learn from you?"

"Not from me, actually. From the past. From history, what other people have thought. I'm really not any more capable than you . . . but I know history, small portions of it. I won't teach you so much, as guide."

"I did use your questions," Prufrax said. "But will I ever need to use them—think that way—again?"

Clevo nodded. "Of course."

—You're quiet.

—She's giving in to him.

—She gave in a long time ago.

—She should be afraid.

—Were you—we—ever really afraid of a challenge?

—No.

—Not Senexi, not forbidden knowledge.

—Someone listens with us. Feel—

Clevo first led her through the history of past wars, judging that was appropriate considering her occupation. She was attentive enough, though her mind wandered; sometimes he was didactic, but she found she didn't mind that much. At no time did his attitude change as they pushed through the tangle of the past. Rather her perception of his attitude changed. Her perception of herself changed.

She saw that in all wars, the first stage was to dehumanize the enemy, reduce the enemy to a lower level so that he might be killed without compunction. When the enemy was not human to begin with, the task was easier. As wars progressed, this tactic frequently led to an underestimation of the enemy, with disastrous consequences. "We aren't exactly underestimating the Senexi," Clevo said. "The overs are too smart for that. But we refuse to understand them, and that could make the war last indefinitely."

"Then why don't the overs see that?"

"Because we're being locked into a pattern. We've been fighting for so long, we've begun to lose ourselves. And it's getting worse." He assumed his didactic tone, and she knew he was reciting something he'd formulated years before and repeated to himself a thousand times. "There is no war so important that to win it, we must destroy our minds."

She didn't agree with that; losing the war with the Senexi would mean extinction, as she understood things.

Most often they met in the single unused weapons blister that had not been damaged. They met when the ship was basking in the real between sponge-space jaunts. He brought memory stores with him in portable modules, and they read, listened, experienced together. She never placed a great deal of importance in the things she learned; her interest was focused on Clevo. Still, she learned.

The rest of her time she spent training. She was aware of a growing isolation from the hawks, which she attributed to her uncertain rank status. Was her genotype going to be preserved or not? The decision hadn't been made. The more she learned, the less she wanted to be singled out for honor. Attracting that sort of attention might be dangerous, she thought. Dangerous to whom, or what, she could not say.

Clevo showed her how hero images had been used to indoctrinate birds and hawks in a standard of behavior that was ideal, not realistic. The results were not always good; some tragic blunders had been made by fighters trying to be more than anyone possibly could or refusing to be flexible.

The war was certainly not a fib. Yet more and more the overs seemed to be treating it as one. Unable to bring about strategic victories against the Senexi, the overs had settled in for a long war of attrition and were apparently bent on adapting all human societies to the effort.

"There are overs we never hear of, who make decisions that shape our entire lives. Soon they'll determine whether or not we're even born, if they don't already."

"That sounds paranoid," she said, trying out a new word and concept she had only recently learned.

"Maybe so."

"Besides, it's been like that for ages—not knowing all our overs."

"But it's getting worse," Clevo said. He showed her the projections he had made. In time, if trends continued unchanged, fighters and all other combatants would be treated more and more mechanically, until they became the machines the overs wished them to be.

—No.

—Quiet. How does he feel toward her?

It was inevitable that as she learned under his tute-

lage, he began to feel responsible for her changes. She
was an excellent fighter. He could never be sure that
what he was doing might reduce her effectiveness.
And yet he had fought well—despite similar changes—
until his billet switch. It had been the overs who had
decided he would be more effective, less disruptive,
elsewhere.

Bitterness over that decision was part of his motive.
The overs had done a foolish thing, putting a fighter
into research. Fighters were tenacious. If the truth was
to be hidden, then fighters were the ones likely to ferret
it out. And pass it on. There was a code among fighters,
seldom revealed to their immediate overs, much less to
the supreme overs parsecs distant in their strategos-
pheres. What one fighter learned that could be of help
to another had to be passed on, even under penalty.
Clevo was simply following that unwritten rule.

Passing on the fact that, at one time, things had
been different. That war changed people, governments, societies, and that societies could effect an
enormous change on their constituents, especially
now—change in their lives, their thinking. Things
could become even more structured. Freedom of fight
was a drug, an illusion—

—No!

used to perpetuate a state of hatred.

"Then why do they keep all the data in stores?" she
asked. "I mean, you study the data, everything becomes obvious."

"There are still important people who think we may
want to find our way back someday. They're afraid
we'll lose our roots, but—"

His face suddenly became peaceful. She reached out to touch him, and he jerked slightly, turning toward her in the blister. "What is it?" she asked.

"It's not organized. We're going to lose the information. Ship overs are going to restrict access more and more. Eventually it'll decay, like some already has in these stores. I've been planning for some time to put it all in a single unit—"

—*He* built the mandate!

"and have the overs place one on every ship, with researchers to tend it. Formalize the loose scheme still in effect, but dying. Right now I'm working on the fringes. At least I'm allowed to work. But soon I'll have enough evidence that they won't be able to argue. Evidence of what happens to societies that try to obscure their histories. They go quite mad. The overs are still rational enough to listen; maybe I'll push it through." He looked out the transparent blister. The stars were smudging to one side as the cruiser began probing for entrances to sponge space. "We'd better get back."

"Where are you going to be when we return? We'll all be transferred."

"That's some time removed. Why do you want to know?"

"I'd like to learn more."

He smiled. "That's not your only reason.

"I don't need someone to tell me what my reasons are," she said testily.

"We're so reluctant," he said. She looked at him sharply, irritated and puzzled. "I mean," he continued, "we're hawks. Comrades. Hawks couple like *that*." He snapped his fingers. "But you and I sneak around it all the time."

Prufrax kept her face blank.

"Aren't you receptive toward me?" he asked, his tone almost teasing.

"You're so damned superior. Stuffy," she snapped.

"Aren't you?"

"It's just that's not all," she said, her tone softening.

"Indeed," he said in a barely audible whisper.

In the distance they heard the alarms.

—It was never any different.

—What?

—Things were never any different before me.

—Don't be silly. It's all here.

—If Clevo made the mandate, then he put it here. It isn't true.

—Why are you upset?

—I don't like hearing that everything I believe is a . . . fib.

—I've never known the difference, I suppose. Eyes-open was never all that real to me. This isn't real, you aren't . . . this is eyes-shut. So why be upset? You and I . . . we aren't even whole people. I feel you. You wish the Zap, you fight, not much else. I'm just a shadow, even compared to you. But she is whole. She loves him. She's less a victim than either of us. So something has to have changed.

—You're saying things have gotten worse.

—If the mandate is a lie, that's all I am. You refuse to accept. I *have* to accept, or I'm even less than a shadow.

—I don't refuse to accept. It's just hard.

—You started it. You thought about love.

—You did!

—Do you know what love is?

—Reception.

They first made love in the weapons blister. It came as no surprise; if anything, they approached it so cautiously they were clumsy. She had become more and more receptive, and he had dropped his guard. It had been quick, almost frantic, far from the orchestrated and drawn-out ballet the hawks prided themselves for. There was no pretense. No need to play the roles of artists interacting. They were depending on each other. The pleasure they exchanged was nothing compared to the emotions involved.

"We're not very good with each other," Prufrax said.

Clevo shrugged. "That's because we're shy."

"Shy?"

He explained. In the past—at various times in the past, because such differences had come and gone many times—making love had been more than a physical exchange or even an expression of comradeship. It had been the acknowledgment of a bond between people.

She listened, half-believing. Like everything else she had heard that kind of love seemed strange, distasteful. What if one hawk was lost, and the other continued to love? It interfered with the hardfought, certainly. But she was also fascinated. Shyness—the fear of one's presentation to another. The hesitation to present truth, or the inward confusion of truth at the awareness that another might be important, more important than one thought possible. That such emotions might have existed at one time, and seem so alien now only emphasized the distance of the past, as Clevo had tried to tell her. And that she felt those emotions only confirmed she was not as far from that past as, for dignity's sake, she might have wished.

Complex emotion was not encouraged either at the Grounds or among hawks on station. Complex emotion degraded complex performance. The simple and direct was desirable.

"But all we seem to do is talk—until now," Prufrax said, holding his hand and examining his fingers one by one. They were very little different from her own, though extended a bit from hawk fingers to give greater versatility with key instruction.

"Talking is the most human thing we can do."

She laughed. "I know what you are," she said, moving up until her eyes were even with his chest. "You're stuffy. You aren't the party type."

"Where'd you learn about parties?"

"You gave me literature to read, I read it. You're an instructor at heart. You make love by telling." She felt peculiar, almost afraid, and looked up at his face. "Not that I don't enjoy your lovemaking, like this. Physical."

"You receive well," he said. "Both ways."

"What we're saying," she whispered, "is not truth-speaking. It's amenity." She turned into the stroke of his hand through her hair. "Amenity is supposed to be decadent. That fellow who wrote about heaven and hell. He would call it a sin."

"Amenity is the recognition that somebody may

see or feel differently than you do. It's the recognition of individuals. You and I, we're part of the end of all that."

"Even if you convince the overs?"

He nodded. "They want to repeat success without risk. New individuals are risky, so they duplicate past success. There will be more and more people, fewer individuals. More of you and me, less of others. The fewer individuals, the fewer stories to tell. The less history. We're part of the death of history."

She floated next to him, trying to blank her mind as she had before, to drive out the nagging awareness he was right. She thought she understood the social structure around her. Things seemed new. She said as much.

"It's a path we're taking," Clevo said. "Not a place we're at."

—It's a place *we're* at. How different are *we?*

—But there's so much history in here. How can it be over for us?

—I've been thinking. Do we know the last event recorded in the mandate?

—Don't, we're drifting from Prufrax now. . . .

Aryz felt himself drifting with them. They swept over countless millennia, then swept back the other way. And it became evident that as much change had been wrapped in one year of the distant past as in a thousand years of the closing entries in the mandate. Clevo's voice seemed to follow them, though they were far from his period, far from Prufrax's record.

"Tyranny is the death of history. We fought the

Senexi until we became like them. No change, youth at an end, old age coming upon us. There is no important change, merely elaborations in the pattern."

—How many times have we been here, then? How many times have we died?

Aryz wasn't sure, now. *Was* this the first time humans had been captured? Had he been told everything by the brood mind? Did the Senexi have no *history,* whatever that was—

The accumulated lives of living, thinking beings. Their actions, thoughts, passions, hopes.

The mandate answered even his confused, nonhuman requests. He could understand action, thought, but not passion or hope. Perhaps without those there was no *history.*

—You have no history, the mutated shape told him. There have been millions like you, even millions like the brood mind. What is the last event recorded in the brood mind that is not duplicated a thousand times over, so close they can be melded together for convenience?

—You understand that? Aryz asked the shape.

—Yes.

—How do you understand—because we made you between human and Senexi?

—Not only that.

The requests of the twin captive and shape were moving them back once more into the past, through the dim gray millennia of repeating ages. History began to manifest again, differences in the record.

* * *

On the way back to Mercior, four skirmishes were fought. Prufrax did well in each. She carried something special with her, a thought she didn't even tell Clevo, and she carried the same thought with her through their last days at the Grounds.

Taking advantage of hawk liberty, she opted a posthardfought residence just outside the Grounds, in the relatively uncrowded Daughter of Cities zone. She wouldn't be returning to fight until several issues had been decided—her status most important among them.

Clevo began making his appeal to the middle overs. He was given Grounds duty to finish his proposals. They could stay together for the time being.

The residence was sixteen square meters in area, not elegant—*natural,* as rentOpts described it. Clevo called it a "garret," inaccurately as she discovered when she looked it up in his memory blocs, but perhaps he was describing the tone.

On the last day she lay in the crook of Clevo's arm. They had done a few hours of nature sleep. He hadn't come out yet, and she looked up at his face, reached up with a hand to feel his arm.

It was different from the arms of others she had been receptive toward. It was unique. The thought amused her. There had never been a reception like theirs. This was the beginning. And if both were to be duplicated, this love, this reception, would be repeated an infinite number of times. Clevo meeting Prufrax, teaching her, opening her eyes.

Somehow, even though repetition contributed to the death of history, she was pleased. This was the secret thought she carried into fight. Each time she

would survive, wherever she was, however many du-
plications down the line. She would receive Clevo,
and he would teach her. If not now—if one or the
other died—then in the future. The death of history
might be a good thing. Love could go on forever.

She had lost even a rudimentary apprehension of
death, even with present pleasure to live for. Her
functions had sharpened. She would please him by
doing all the things he could not. And if he was to enter that state she frequently found him in, that state of
introspection, of reliving his own battles and of envy-
ing her activity, then that wasn't bad. All they did to
each other was good.

—*Was* good

—*Was*

She slipped from his arm and left the narrow sleeping quarter, pushing through the smoke-colored air
curtain to the lounge. Two hawks and an over she had
never seen before were sitting there. They looked up
at her.

"Under," Prufrax said.

"Over," the woman returned. She was dressed in
tan and green, Grounds colors, not ship.

"May I assist?"

"Yes."

"My duty, then?"

The over beckoned her closer. "You have been receiving a researcher."

"Yes," Prufrax said. The meetings could not have
been a secret on the ship, and certainly not their
quartering near the Grounds. "Has that been against
duty?"

"No." The over eyed Prufrax sharply, observing her perfected fightform, the easy grace with which she stood, naked, in the middle of the small compartment. "But a decision has been reached. Your status is decided now."

She felt a shiver.

"Prufrax," said the elder hawk. She recognized him from fibs, and his companion: Kumnax and Arol. Once her heroes. "You have been accorded an honor, just as your partner has. You have a valuable genetic assortment—"

She barely heard the rest. They told her she would return to fight, until they deemed she had had enough experience and background to be brought into the polinstruc division. Then her fighting would be over. She would serve better as an example, a hero.

Heroes never partnered out of function. Hawk heroes could not even partner with exhawks.

Clevo emerged from the air curtain. "Duty," the over said. "The residence is disbanded. Both of you will have separate quarters, separate duties."

They left. Prufrax held out her hand, but Clevo didn't take it. "No use," he said.

Suddenly she was filled with anger. "You'll give it up? Did I expect too much? *How strongly?*"

"Perhaps even more strongly than you," he said. "I knew the order was coming down. And still I didn't leave. That may hurt my chances with the supreme overs."

"Then at least I'm worth more than your breeding history?"

"Now you are history. History the way they make it."

"I feel like I'm dying," she said, amazement in her voice. "What is that, Clevo? What did you do to me?"

"I'm in pain, too," he said.

"You're hurt?"

"I'm confused."

"I don't believe that," she said, her anger rising again. "You knew, and you didn't do anything?"

"That would have been counter to duty. We'll be worse off if we fight it."

"So what good is your great, exalted history?"

"History is what you have," Clevo said. "I only record."

—Why did they separate them?

—I don't know. You didn't like him, anyway.

—Yes, but now . . .

—See? You're her. We're her. But shadows. She was whole.

—I don't understand.

—We don't. Look what happens to her. They took what was best out of her. Prufrax

went into battle eighteen more times before dying as heroes often do, dying in the midst of what she did best. The question of what made her better before the separation—for she definitely was not as fine a fighter after—has not been settled. Answers fall into an extinct classification of knowledge, and there are few left to interpret, none accessible to this device.

—So she went out and fought and died. They never even made fibs about her. This killed her?

—I don't think so. She fought well enough. She died like other hawks died.

—And she might have lived otherwise.

—How can I know that, any more than you?

—They—we—met again, you know. I met a Clevo once, on my ship. They didn't let me stay with him long.

—How did you react to him?

—There was so little time, I don't know.

—Let's ask. . . .

In thousands of duty stations, it was inevitable that some of Prufrax's visions would come true, that they should meet now and then. Clevos were numerous, as were Prufraxes. Every ship carried complements of several of each. Though Prufrax was never quite as successful as the original, she was a fine type. She—

—She was never quite as successful. They took away her edge. They didn't even know it!

—They must have known.

—Then they didn't want to win!

—We don't know that. Maybe there were more important considerations.

—Yes, like killing history.

Aryz shuddered in his warming body, dizzy as if about to bud, then regained control. He had been pulled from the mandate, called to his own duty.

He examined the shapes and the human captive. There was something different about them. How long had they been immersed in the mandate? He checked quickly, frantically, before answering the call. The reconstructed Mam had malfunctioned. None of them had been nourished. They were thin, pale, cooling.

Even the bloated mutant shape was dying; lost, like the others, in the mandate.

He turned his attention away. Everything was confusion. Was he human or Senexi now? Had he fallen so low as to understand them? He went to the origin of the call, the ruins of the temporary brood chamber. The corridors were caked with ammonia ice, burning his pod as he slipped over them. The brood mind had come out of flux bind. The emergency support systems hadn't worked well; the brood mind was damaged.

"Where have you been?" it asked.

"I assumed I would not be needed until your return from the flux bind."

"You have not been watching!"

"Was there any need? We are so advanced in time, all our actions are obsolete. The nebula is collapsed, the issue is decided."

"We do not know that. We are being pursued."

Aryz turned to the sensor wall—what was left of it—and saw that they were, indeed, being pursued. He had been lax.

"It is not your fault," the brood mind said. "You have been set a task that tainted you and ruined your function. You will dissipate."

Aryz hesitated. He had become so different, so tainted, that he actually *hesitated* at a direct command from the brood mind. But it was damaged. Without him, without what he had learned, what could it do? It wasn't reasoning correctly.

"There are facts you must know, important facts—"

Aryz felt a wave of revulsion, uncomprehending fear, and something not unlike human anger radiate from the brood mind. Whatever he had learned and however he had changed, he could not withstand that wave.

Willingly, and yet against his will—it didn't matter––he felt himself liquefying. His pod slumped beneath him, and he fell over, landing on a pool of frozen ammonia. It burned, but he did not attempt to lift himself. Before he ended, he saw with surprising clarity what it was to be a branch ind, or a brood mind, or a human. Such a valuable insight, and it leaked out of his permea and froze on the ammonia.

The brood mind regained what control it could of the fragment. But there were no defenses worthy of the name. Calm, preparing for its own dissipation, it waited for the pursuit to conclude.

The Mam set off an alarm. The interface with the mandate was severed. Weak, barely able to crawl, the humans looked at each other in horror and slid to opposite corners of the chamber.

They were confused: which of them was the captive, which the decoy shape? It didn't seem important. They were both bone-thin, filthy with their own excrement. They turned with one motion to stare at the bloated mutant. It sat in its corner, tiny head incongruous on the huge thorax, tiny arms and legs barely functional even when healthy. It smiled wanly at them.

"We felt you," one of the Prufraxes said. "You were with us in there." Her voice was a soft croak.

"That was my place," it replied. "My only place."

"What function, what name?"

"I'm . . . I know that. I'm a researcher. In there. I knew myself in there."

They squinted at the shape. The head. Something familiar, even now. "You're a Clevo . . ."

There was noise all around them, cutting off the shape's weak words. As they watched, their chamber was sectioned like an orange, and the wedges peeled open. The illumination ceased. Cold enveloped them.

A naked human female, surrounded by tiny versions of herself, like an angel circled by fairy kin, floated into the chamber. She was thin as a snake. She wore nothing but silver rings on her wrists and a narrow torque around her waist. She glowed blue-green in the dark.

The two Prufraxes moved their lips weakly but made no sound in the near vacuum. *Who are you?*

She surveyed them without expression, then held out her arms as if to fly. She wore no gloves, but she was of their type.

As she had done countless times before on finding such Senexi experiments—though this seemed older than most—she lifted one arm higher. The blue-green intensified, spread in waves to the mangled walls, surrounded the freezing, dying shapes. Perfect, angelic, she left the debris behind to cast its fitful glow and fade.

They had destroyed every portion of the fragment but one. They left it behind unharmed.

Then they continued, millions of them thick like mist, working the spaces between the stars, their only master the overness of the real.

They needed no other masters. They would never malfunction.

The mandate drifted in the dark and cold, its memory going on, but its only life the rapidly fading tracks where minds had once passed through it. The trails writhed briefly, almost as if alive, but only following the quantum rules of diminishing energy states. Finally, a small memory was illuminated.

Prufrax's last poem, explained the mandate reflexively.

> *How the fires grow! Peace passes*
> *All memory lost.*
> *Somehow we always miss that single door*
> *Dooming ourselves to circle.*
>
> *Ashes to stars, lies to souls,*
> *Let's spin round the sinks and holes.*
>
> *Kill the good, eat the young.*
> *Forever and more*
> *You and I are never done.*

The track faded into nothing. Around the mandate, the universe grew old very quickly.

SCATTERSHOT

The teddy bear spoke excellent mandarin. It stood about fifty centimeters tall, a plump fellow with close-set eyes above a nose unusually long for the generally pug breed. It paced around me, muttering to itself.

I rolled over and felt barbs down my back and sides. My arms moved with reluctance. Something about my will to get up and the way my muscles reacted was out-of-kilter; the nerves didn't conveying properly. So it was, I thought, with my eyes and the small black-and-white beast they claimed to see: a derangement of phosphene patterns, cross-tied with childhood memories and snatches of linguistics courses ten years past.

It began speaking Russian. I ignored it and focused on other things. The rear wall of my cabin was unrecognizable, covered with geometric patterns that shifted in and out of bas-relief and glowed faintly in the shadow cast by a skewed panel light. My foldout desk had been torn from its hinges and now lay on the floor, not far from my head. The ceiling was cream-colored. Last I remembered it had been a pleasant shade of burnt orange. Thus tallied, half my cabin was still with me. The other half had been ferried away in the—

Disruption. I groaned, and the bear stepped back nervously. My body was gradually coordinating. Bits and pieces of disassembled vision integrated and stopped their random flights, and still the creature walked, and still it spoke, though getting deep into German.

It was not a minor vision. It was either real or a full-fledged hallucination.

"What's going on?" I asked.

It bent over me, sighed, and said, "Of all the fated arrangements. A speaking I know not the best of— Anglo." It held out its arms and shivered. "Pardon the distraught. My cords of psyche—nerves?—they have not decided which continuum to obey this moment."

"Same for me," I said cautiously. "Who are you?"

"Psyche, we are all psyche. Take this care and be not content with illusion, this path, this merriment. Excuse. Some writers in English. All I know is from the read."

"Am I still on my ship?"

"So we are all, and *hors de combat.* We limp for the duration."

I was integrated enough to stand, and I towered over the bear, rearranging my tunic. My left breast ached with a bruise. Because we had been riding at one G for five days, I was wearing a bra, and the bruise lay directly under a strap. Such, to quote, was the fated arrangement. As my wits gathered and held converse, I considered what might have happened and felt a touch of the "distraughts" myself. I began to shiver like a recruit in pressure-drop training.

We had survived. That is, at least I had survived, out of a crew of forty-three. How many others?

"Do you know . . . have you found out—"

"Worst," the bear said. "Some I do not catch, the deciphering of other things not so hard. Disrupted about seven, eight hours past. It was a force of many, for I have counted ten separate things not in my recognition." It grinned. "You are ten, and best yet. We are perhaps not so far in world-lines."

We'd been told survival after disruption was possible. Practical statistics indicated one out of myriad ships, so struck, would remain integral. For a weapon that didn't actually kill in itself, the probability disrupter was very effective.

"Are we intact?" I asked.

"Fated," the Teddy bear said. "I cognize we can even move and seek a base. Depending."

"Depending," I echoed. The creature sounded masculine, despite size and a childlike voice. "Are you a he? Or—"

"He," the bear said quickly.

I touched the bulkhead above the door and ran my finger along a familiar, slightly crooked seam. Had the disruption kept me in my own universe—against incalculable odds—or exchanged me to some other? Was either of us in a universe we could call our own?

"Is it safe to look around?"

The bear hummed. "Cognize—know not. Last I saw, others had not reached a state of organizing."

It was best to start from the beginning. I looked down at the creature and rubbed a bruise on my forehead. "Wh-where are you from?"

"Same as you, possible," he said. "Earth. Was mascot to captain, for cuddle and advice."

That sounded bizarre enough. I walked to the hatchway and peered down the corridor. It was plain and utilitarian, but neither the right color nor configuration. The hatch at the end was round and had a manual sealing system, six black throw-bolts that no human engineer would ever have put on a spaceship. "What's your name?"

"Have got no official name. Mascot name known only to captain."

I was scared, so my brusque nature surfaced and I asked him sharply if his captain was in sight, or any other aspect of the world he'd known.

"Cognize not," he answered. "Call me Sonok."

"I'm Geneva," I said. "Francis Geneva."

"We are friends?"

"I don't see why not. I hope we're not the only ones who can be friendly. Is English difficult for you?"

"Mind not. I learn fast. Practice make perfection."

"Because I can speak some Russian, if you want."

"Good as I with Anglo?" Sonok asked. I detected a sense of humor—and self-esteem—in the bear.

"No, probably not. English it is. If you need to know anything, don't be embarrassed to ask."

"Sonok hardly embarrassed by anything. Was mascot."

The banter was providing a solid framework for my sanity to grab on to. I had an irrational desire to take the bear and hug him, just for want of something warm. His attraction was undeniable—tailored, I guessed, for that very purpose. But tailored from what? The color suggested panda; the shape did not.

"What do you think we should do?" I asked, sitting on my bunk.

"Sonok not known for quick decisions," he said, squatting on the floor in front of me. He was stubby-limbed but far from clumsy.

"Nor am I," I said. "I'm a software and machinery language expert. I wasn't combat-trained."

"Not cognize 'software,'" Sonok said.

"Programming materials," I explained. The bear nodded and got up to peer around the door. He pulled back and scrabbled to the rear of the cabin.

"They're here!" he said. "Can port shut?"

"I wouldn't begin to know how—" But I retreated just as quickly and clung to my bunk. A stream of serpents flowed by the hatchway, metallic green and yellow, with spade-shaped heads and red ovals running dorsally.

The stream passed without even a hint of intent to molest, and Sonok climbed down the bas-relief pattern. "What the hell are they doing here?" I asked.

"They are a crew member, I think," Sonok said.

154

"What—who else is out there?"

The bear straightened and looked at me steadily. "Have none other than to seek," he said solemnly. "Elsewise, we possess no rights to ask. No?" The bear walked to the hatch, stepped over the bottom seal, and stood in the corridor. "Come?"

I got up and followed.

A woman's mind is a strange pool to slip into at birth. It is set within parameters by the first few months of listening and seeing. Her infant mind is a vast blank template that absorbs all and stores it away. In those first few months come role acceptance, a beginning to attitude, and a hint of future achievement. Listening to adults and observing their actions build a storehouse of preconceptions and warnings: *Do not see those ghosts on bedroom walls—they aren't there! None of the rest of us can see your imaginary companions, darling. . . . It's something you have to understand.*

And so, from some dim beginning, not *ex nihilo* but out of totality, the woman begins to pare her infinite self down. She whittles away at this unwanted piece, that undesired trait. She forgets in time that she was once part of all and turns to the simple tune of life, rather than to the endless and symphonic *before*. She forgets those companions who danced on the ceiling above her bed and called to her from the dark. Some of them were friendly; others, even in the dim time, were not pleasant. But they were all *she*. For the rest of her life, the woman seeks some echo of that preternatural menagerie; in the men she chooses to love, in the tasks she chooses to perform, in the way she tries to be. After thirty years of cutting, she becomes Francis Geneva.

When love dies, another piece is pared away, another universe is sheared off, and the split can never join again. With each winter and spring, spent on or off worlds with or without seasons, the woman's life grows more solid, and smaller.

But now the parts are coming together again, the companions out of the dark above the child's bed. Beware of them. They're all the things you once lost or let go, and now they walk on their own, out of your control; reborn, as it were, and indecipherable.

"Do you have understanding?" the bear asked. I shook my head to break my steady stare at the six-bolted hatch.

"Understand what?" I asked.

"Of how we are here."

"Disrupted. By Aighors, I presume."

"Yes, they are the ones for us, too. But how?"

"I don't know," I said. No one did. We could only observe the results. When the remains of disrupted ships could be found, they always resembled floating garbage heaps—plucked from our universe, rearranged in some cosmic grab bag, and returned. What came back was of the same mass, made up of the same basic materials, and recombined with a tendency toward order and viability. But in deep space, even ninety percent viability was tantamount to none at all. If the ship's separate elements didn't integrate perfectly—a one in a hundred thousand chance—there were no survivors. But oh, how interested we were in the corpses! Most were kept behind the Paper Curtain of secrecy, but word leaked out even so—word of ostriches with large heads, blobs with bits of crystalline seawater still adhering to them . . . and now my own additions, a living Teddy bear and a herd of particolored snakes. All had been snatched out of terrestrial ships from a maze of different universes.

Word also leaked out that of five thousand such incidents, not once had a human body been returned to our continuum.

"Some things still work," Sonok said. 'We are heavy the same."

The gravitation was unchanged—I hadn't paid attention to that. 'We can still breathe, for that matter," I said. 'We're all from one world. There's no reason to think the basics will change." And that meant there had to be standards for communication, no matter how diverse the forms. Communication was part of my expertise, but thinking about it made me shiver. A ship runs on computers, or their equivalent. How were at least ten different computer systems communicating? Had they integrated with working interfaces? If they hadn't, our time was limited. Soon all hell would join us, darkness and cold, and vacuum.

I released the six throw-bolts and opened the hatch slowly.

"Say, Geneva," Sonok mused as we looked into the

corridor beyond. "How did the snakes get through here?"

I shook my head. There were more important problems. "I want to find something like a ship's bridge, or at least a computer terminal. Did you see something before you found my cabin?"

Sonok nodded. "Other way in corridor. But there were . . . things there. Didn't enjoy the looks, so came this way."

"What were they?" I asked.

"One like trash can," he said. "With breasts."

"We'll keep looking this way," I said by way of agreement.

The next bulkhead was a dead end. A few round displays studded the wall, filled like bull's-eyes with concentric circles of varying thickness. A lot of information could be carried in such patterns, given a precise optical scanner to read them—which suggested a machine more than an organism, though not necessarily. The bear paced back and forth in front of the wall.

I reached out with one hand to touch the displays. Then I got down on my knees to feel the bulkhead, looking for a seam. "Can't see it, but I feel something here—like a ridge in the material."

The bulkhead, displays and all, peeled away like a heart's triplet valve, and a rush of air shoved us into darkness. I instinctively rolled into a fetal curl. The bear bumped against me and grabbed my arm. Some throbbing force flung us this way and that, knocking us against squeaking wet things. I forced my eyes open and unfurled my arms and legs, trying to find a grip. One hand rapped against metal or hard plastic, and the other caught what felt like rope. With some fumbling, I gripped the rope and braced myself against the hard surface. Then I had time to sort out what I was seeing. The chamber seemed to be open to space, but we were breathing, so obviously a transparent membrane was keeping in the atmosphere. I could see the outer surface of the ship, and it appeared a hell of a lot larger than I'd allowed. Clinging to the membrane in a curve, as though queued on the inside of a bubble, were five or six round nebulosities that glowed dull orange like dying suns. I was hanging on to something resembling a ship's mast, a metal pylon that reached from one side of the valve to the center of the bubble. Ropes were rigged from the pylon to stanchions that seemed suspended in midair, though they had to be secured against the membrane. The ropes and pylon supported clusters of head-sized spheres covered with hairlike plastic tubing. They clucked like brood hens as they slid away from us. "Góspodi!" Sonok screeched.

The valve that had given us access was still open, pushing its flaps in and out. I kicked away from the pylon. The bear's grip was fierce. The flaps loomed, slapped against us, and closed with a final sucking throb. We were on the other side, lying on the floor. The bulkhead again was impassively blank.

The bear rolled away from my arm and stood up. "Best to try the other way!" he suggested. "More easily faced, I cognize."

I unshipped the six-bolted hatch, and we crawled through. We doubled back and went past my cabin.

The corridor, now that I thought of it, was strangely naked. In any similar region on my ship there would have been pipes, access panels, printed instructions and at least ten cabin doors.

The corridor curved a few yards past my cabin, and the scenery became more diverse. We found several small cubbyholes, all empty, and Sonok walked cautiously ahead. "Here," he said. "Can was here."

"Gone now," I observed. We stepped through another six-bolt hatch into a chamber that had the vague appearance of a command center. In large details it resembled the bridge of my own ship, and I rejoiced for that small sense of security.

"Can you talk to it?" Sonok asked.

"I can try. But where's a terminal?"

The bear pointed to a curved bench in front of a square, flat surface, devoid of keyboard, speaker, or knobs. It didn't look much like a terminal—though the flat surface resembled a visual display screen—but I wasn't ashamed to try speaking to it. Nor was I abashed when it didn't answer. "No go. Something else."

We looked around the chamber for several minutes but found nothing more promising. "It's like a bridge," I said, "but nothing matches specifically. Maybe we're looking for the wrong thing."

"Machines run themselves, perhaps," Sonok suggested.

I sat on the bench, resting an elbow on the edge of the "screen." Nonhuman technologies frequently use other senses for information exchange than we do. Where we generally limit machine-human interactions to sight, sound, and sometimes touch, the Crocerians use odor, and the Aighors control their machines on occasion with microwave radiation from their nervous systems. I laid my hand across the screen. It was warm to the touch, but I couldn't detect any variation in the warmth. Infrared was an inefficient carrier of information for creatures with visual orientation. Snakes use infrared to seek their prey—

"Snakes," I said. "The screen is warm. Is this part of the snake ship?"

Sonok shrugged. I looked around the cabin to find other smooth surfaces. They were few. Most were crisscrossed with raised grills. Some were warm to the touch. There were any number of possibilities—but I doubted if I would hit on the right one very quickly. The best I could hope for was the survival of some other portion of my ship.

"Sonok, is there another way out of this room?"

"Several. One is around the gray pillar," he said. "Another hatch with six dogs."

"What?"

"Six . . ." He made a grabbing motion with one hand. "Like the others."

"Throw-bolts," I said.

"I thought my Anglo was improving," he muttered sulkily.

"It is. But it's bound to be different from mine, so we both have to adapt." We opened the hatch and looked into the next chamber. The lights flickered feebly, and wrecked equipment gave off acrid smells. A haze of cloying smoke drifted out and immediately set ventilators to work. The bear held his nose and jumped over the seal for a quick walk through the room.

"Is something dead in here," he said when he returned. "Not like human, but not far. It is shot in head." He nodded for me to go with him, and I reluctantly followed. The body was pinned between two bolted seats. The head was a mess, and there was ample evidence that it used red blood. The body was covered by gray overalls and, though twisted into an awkward position, was obviously more canine than human. The bear was correct in one respect: it was closer to me than whiskered balls or rainbow snakes. The smoke was almost clear when I stepped back from the corpse.

"Sonok, any possibility this could be another mascot?"

The bear shook his head and walked away, nose wrinkled. I wondered if I'd insulted him.

"I see nothing like terminal here," he said. "Looks like nothing work now, anyway. Go on?"

We returned to the bridgelike chamber, and Sonok picked out another corridor. By the changing floor curvature, I guessed that all my previous estimates as to ship size were appreciably off. There was no way of telling either the shape or the size of this collage of vessels. What I'd seen from the bubble had appeared endless, but that might have been optical distortion.

The corridor dead-ended again, and we didn't press our luck as to what lay beyond the blank bulkhead. As we turned back, I asked, "What were the things you saw? You said there were ten of them, all different."

The bear held up his paws and counted. His fingers were otterlike and quite supple. "Snakes, number one," he said. "Cans with breasts, two; back wall of your cabin, three; blank bulkhead with circular marks, four; and you, five. Other things not so different, I think now snakes and six-dog hatches might go together, since snakes know how to use them. Other things—you and your cabin fixtures, so on, all together. But you add dead thing in overalls, fuzzy balls, and who can say where it ends?"

"I hope it ends someplace. I can only face so many variations before I give up. Is there anything left of your ship?"

"Where I was after disruption," the bear said. "On my stomach in bathroom."

Ah, that blessed word! "Where?" I asked. "Is it working?" I'd considered impolitely messing the corridors if there was no alternative.

"Works still, I think. Back through side corridor."

He showed me the way. A lot can be learned from a bathroom social attitudes, technological levels, even basic psychology, not to mention anatomy. This one was lovely and utilitarian, with fixtures for males and females of at least three sizes. I made do with the largest. The bear gave me privacy, which wasn't strictly necessary—bathrooms on my ship being coed—but appreciated, nonetheless. Exposure to a Teddy bear takes getting used to.

When I was through, I joined Sonok in the hall and realized I'd gotten myself turned around. "Where are we?"

"Is changing," Sonok said. "Where bulkhead was, is now hatch. I'm not sure I cognize how—it's a different hatch."

And it was, in an alarming way. It was battle-armored, automatically controlled, and equipped with heavily shielded detection equipment. It was ugly and khaki-colored and had no business being inside a ship, unless the occupants distrusted each other. "I was in anteroom, outside lavatory," Sonok said, "with door closed. I hear loud sound and something like metal being cut, and I open door to see this."

Vague sounds of machines were still audible, grinding and screaming. We stayed away from the hatch. Sonok motioned for me to follow him. "One more," he said. "Almost forgot." He pointed into a cubbyhole, about a meter deep and two meters square. "Look like fish tank, perhaps?"

It was a large rectangular tank filled with murky fluid. It reached from my knees to the top of my head and fit the cubbyhole perfectly. "Hasn't been cleaned, in any case," I said.

I touched the glass to feel how warm or cold it was. The tank lighted up, and I jumped back, knocking Sonok over. He rolled into a backward flip and came upright, wheezing.

The light in the tank flickered like a strobe, gradually speeding up until the glow was steady. For a few seconds it made me dizzy. The murk was gathering itself together. I bent over cautiously to get a close look. The murk wasn't evenly distributed. It was composed of animals like brine shrimp no more than a centimeter long, with two black eyespots at one end, a pinkish "spine," and a feathery fringe rippling between head and tail. They were forming a dense mass at the center of the tank.

Ordered dots of luminescence crossed the bottom of the tank, changing colors across a narrow spectrum: red, blue, amber.

"It's doing something," Sonok said. The mass was defining a shape. Shoulders and head appeared, then torso and arms, sculpted in ghost-colored brine shrimp. When the living sculpture was finished, I recognized myself from the waist up. I held out my arm, and the mass slowly followed suit.

I had an inspiration. In my pants pocket I had a marker for labeling tapas cube blanks. It used soft plastic wrapped in a metal jacket. I took it out and wrote three letters across the transparent front of the tank: WHO. Part of the mass dissolved and re-formed to mimic the letters, the rest filling in behind. WHO they spelled, then they added a question mark.

Sonok chirped, and I came closer to see better. "They understand?" he asked. I shook my head. I had no idea what I was playing with. WHAT ARE YOU? I wrote.

The animals started to break up and return to the general murk. I shook my head in frustration. So near! The closest thing to communication yet.

"Wait," Sonok said. "They're group again."

TENZIONA, the shrimp coalesced. DYSFUNCTIO. GUARDATEO AB PEREGRINO PERAMBULA.

"I don't understand. Sounds like Italian—do you know any Italian?"

The bear shook his head.

"'Dysfunctio,'" I read aloud. "That seems plain enough. '*Ab peregrino*'? Something about a hawk?"

"*Peregrine,* it is foreigner," Sonok said.

"Guard against foreigners . . . 'perambula,' as in strolling? Watch for the foreigners who walk? Well, we don't have the grammar, but it seems to tell us something we already know. Christ! I wish I could remember all the languages they filled me with ten years ago."

The marks on the tank darkened and flaked off. The shrimp began to form something different. They grouped into branches and arranged themselves nose-to-tail, upright, to form a trunk, which rooted itself to the floor of the tank.

"Tree," Sonok said.

Again they dissolved, returning in a few seconds to the simulacrum of my body. The clothing seemed different, however—more like a robe. Each shrimp changed its individual color now, making the shape startlingly lifelike. As I watched, the image began to age. The outlines of the face sagged, wrinkles formed in the skin, and the limbs shrank perceptibly. My arms felt cold, and I crossed them over my breasts; but the corridor was reasonably warm.

* * *

Of course the universe isn't really held in a little girl's mind. It's one small thread in a vast skein, separated from every other universe by a limitation of constants and qualities, just as death is separated from life by the eternal nonreturn of the dead. Well, now we know the universes are less inviolable than death, for there are ways of crossing from thread to thread. So these other beings, from similar Earths, are not part of my undifferentiated infancy. That's a weak fantasy for a rather unequipped young woman to indulge in. Still, the symbols of childhood lie all around—nightmares and Teddy bears and dreams held in a tank; dreams of old age and death. And a tree, gray and ghostly, without leaves. That's me. Full of winter, wood cracking into splinters. How do they know?

A rustling came from the corridor ahead. We turned from the tank and saw the floor covered with rainbow snakes, motionless, all heads aimed at us. Sonok began to tremble.

"Stop it," I said. "They haven't done anything to us."

"You are bigger," he said. "Not meal-sized."

"They'd have a rough time putting you away, too. Let's just sit it out calmly and see what this is all about." I kept my eyes on the snakes and away from the tank. I didn't want to see the shape age any more. For all the sanity of this place, it might have kept on going, through death and decay down to bones. Why did it choose me; why not Sonok?

"I cannot wait," Sonok said. "I have not the patience of a snake." He stepped forward. The snakes watched without a sound as the bear approached, one step every few seconds. "I want to know one solid thing," he called back. "Even if it is whether they eat small furry mascots."

The snakes suddenly bundled backward and started to crawl over each other. Small sucking noises smacked between their bodies. As they crossed, the red ovals met and held firm. They assembled and reared into a single mass, cobralike, but flat as a planarian worm. A fringe of snakes weaved across the belly like a caterpillar's idea of Medusa.

Brave Sonok was undone. He swung around and ran past me. I was too shocked to do anything but face the snakes down, neck hairs crawling. I wanted to speak but couldn't. Then, behind me, I heard: "Sinieux!"

As I turned, I saw two things, one in the corner of each eye: the snakes fell into a pile, and a man dressed in red and black vanished into a side corridor. The snakes regrouped into a hydra with six tentacles and grasped the hatch's throw-bolts, springing it open and slithering through. The hatch closed, and I was alone.

There was nothing for it but to scream a moment, then cry. I lay back against the wall, getting the fit out of me as loudly and quickly as possible. When I was able to stop, I wiped my eyes with my palms and kept them covered, feeling ashamed. When I looked out again, Sonok stood next to me.

"We've an Indian on board," he said. "Big, with black hair in three ribbons"—he motioned from crown to neck between his ears—"and a snappy dresser."

"Where is he?" I asked hoarsely.

"Back in place like bridge, I think. He controls snakes?"

I hesitated, then nodded.

"Go look?"

I got up and followed the bear. Sitting on a bench pulled from the wall, the man in red and black watched us as we entered the chamber. He was big—at least two meters tall—and hefty, dressed in a black silk shirt with red cuffs. His cape was black with a red eagle embroidered across the shoulders. He certainly looked Indian—ruddy skin, aristocratic nose, full lips held tight as if against pain.

"*Quis la?*" he queried.

"I don't speak that," I said. "Do you know English?"

The Indian didn't break his stolid expression. He nodded and turned on the bench to put his hand against a grill. "I was taught in the British school at Nova London," he said, his accent distinctly Oxfordian. "I was educated in Indonesia, and so I speak Dutch, High and Middle German, and some Asian tongues, specifically Nippon and Tagalog. But at English I am fluent."

"Thank God," I said. "Do you know this room?"

"Yes," he replied. "I designed it. It's for the Sinieux."

"Do you know what's happened to us?"

"We have fallen into hell," he said. "My Jesuit professors warned me of it."

"Not far wrong," I said. "Do you know why?"

"I do not question my punishments."

"We're not being punished—at least, not by God or devils."

He shrugged. It was a moot point.

"I'm from Earth, too," I said. "From Terre."

"I know the words for Earth," the Indian said sharply.

"But I don't think it's the same Earth. What year are you from? Since he'd mentioned Jesuits, he almost had to use the standard Christian Era dating.

"Year of Our Lord 2345," he said.

Sonok crossed himself elegantly. "For me 2290," he added. The Indian examined the bear dubiously.

I was sixty years after the bear, five after the Indian. The limits of the grab bag were less hazy now. "What country?"

"Alliance of Tribal Columbia," he answered, "District Quebec, East Shore."

"I'm from the Moon," I said. "But my parents were born on Earth in the United States of America."

The Indian shook his head slowly; he wasn't familiar with it.

"Was there—" But I held back the question. Where to begin? Where did the world-lines part? "I think we'd better consider finding out how well this ship is put together. We'll get into our comparative histories later. Obviously you have star drive."

The Indian didn't agree or disagree. "My parents had ancestors from the West Shore, Vancouver," he said. "They were Kwakiutl and Kodikin. The animal, does it have a Russian accent?"

"Some," I said. "It's better than it was a few hours ago."

170

"I have blood debts against Russians."

"Okay," I said, "but I doubt if you have anything against this one considering the distances involved. We've got to learn if this ship can take us someplace."

"I have asked," he said.

"Where?" Sonok asked. "A terminal?"

"The ship says it is surrounded by foreign parts and can barely understand them. But it can get along."

"You really don't know what happened, do you?"

"I went to look for worlds for my people and took the Sinieux with me. When I reached a certain coordinate in the sky, far along the arrow line established by my extrasolar pierce, this happened." He lifted his hand. "Now there is one creature, a devil, that tried to attack me. It is dead. There are others, huge black men who wear golden armor and carry gold guns like cannon, and they have gone away behind armored hatches. There are walls like rubber that open onto more demons. And now you—and it." He pointed at the bear.

"I'm not an 'it,'" Sonok said. "I'm an ours."

"Small ours," the Indian retorted.

Sonok bristled and turned away. "Enough," I said. "You haven't fallen into hell, not literally. We've been hit by something called a disrupter. It snatched us from different universes and reassembled us according to our world-lines, our . . . affinities."

The Indian smiled faintly, very condescendingly.

"Listen, do you understand how crazy this is?" I demanded, exasperated. "I've got to get things straight before we all lose our calm. The beings who did this—in my universe they're called 'Aighors.' Do you know about them?"

He shook his head. "i know of no other beings but those of Earth. I went to look for worlds."

"Is your ship a warper ship—does it travel across a geodesic in higher spaces?"

"Yes," he said. "It is not in phase with the crest of the Stellar Sea but slips between the foamy length, where we must struggle to obey all laws."

That was a fair description of translating from status geometry—our universe—to higher geometries. It was more poetic than scientific, but he was here, so it worked well enough. "How long have your people been able to travel this way?"

"Ten years. And yours?"

"Three centuries."

He nodded in appreciation. "You know then what you speak of, and perhaps there aren't any devils, and we are not in hell. Not this time."

"How do you use your instruments in here?"

"I do not, generally. The Sinieux use them. If you will not get upset, I'll demonstrate."

I glanced at Sonok, who was still sulking. "Are you afraid of the snakes?"

The bear shook his head.

"Bring them in," I said. "And perhaps we should know each other's name?"

"Jean Frobish," the Indian said. And I told him mine.

The snakes entered at his whistled command and assembled in the middle of the cabin. There were two sets, each made up of about fifty. When meshed, they made two formidable metaserpents. Frobish instructed them with spoken commands and a language that sounded like birdcalls. Perfect servants, they obeyed faultlessly and without hesitation. They went to the controls at his command and made a few manipulations, then turned to him and delivered, one group at a time, a report in consonantal hisses and claps. The exchange was uncanny and chilling. Jean nodded, and the serpents disassembled.

"Are they specially bred?" I asked.

"Tectonogenetic farming," he said. "They are excellent workers and have no will of their own, since they have no cerebrums. They can remember, and en masse can think, but not for themselves, if you see what I mean." He showed another glimmer of a smile. He was proud of his servants.

"I think I understand. Sonok, were you specially bred?"

"Was mascot," Sonok said. "Could breed for myself, given chance."

The subject was touchy, I could see. I could also see that Frobish and Sonok wouldn't get along without friction. If Sonok had been a big bear—and not a Russian—instead of an ursine dwarf, the Indian might have had more respect for him.

"Jean, can you command the whole ship from here?"

"Those parts that answer."

"Can your computers tell you how much of the ship will respond?"

"What is left of my vessel responds very well. The rest is balky or blank entirely. I was trying to discover the limits when I encountered you."

"You met the people who've been putting in the armored hatches?'

He nodded. "Bigger than Masai," he said.

I now had explanations for some of the things we'd seen and could link them with terrestrial origins. Jean and his Sinieux weren't beyond the stretch of reason, nor was Sonok. The armored hatches weren't quite as mysterious now. But what about the canine? I swallowed. That must have been the demon Frobish killed. And beyond the triplet valves?

"We've got a lot to find out," I said.

"You and the animal, are you together, from the same world?" Frobish asked. I shook my head. "Did you come alone?"

I nodded. "Why?"

"No men, no soldiers?"

I was apprehensive now. "No."

"Good." He stood and approached a blank wall near the gray pillar. "Then we will not have too many to support, unless the ones in golden armor want our food." He put his hand against the wall, and a round opening appeared. In the shadow of the hole, two faces watched with eyes glittering.

"These are my wives," Frobish said. One was dark-haired and slender, no more than fifteen or sixteen. She stepped out first and looked at me warily. The second, stockier and flatter of face, was brown-haired and about twenty. Frobish pointed to the younger first. "This is Alouette," he said. "And this is Mouse. Wives, acquaint with Francis Geneva." They stood one on each side of Frobish, holding his elbows, and nodded at me in unison.

That made four humans, more if the blacks in golden armor were men. Our collage had hit the jackpot.

"Jean, you say your machines can get along with the rest of the ship. Can they control it? If they can, I think we should try to return to Earth."

"To what?" Sonok asked. "Which Earth waits?"

"What's the bear talking about?" Frobish asked.

I explained the situation as best I could. Frobish was a sophisticated engineer and astrogator, but his experience with other continua—theoretical or actual—was small. He tightened his lips and listened grimly, unwilling to admit his ignorance. I sighed and looked to Alouette and Mouse for support. They were meek, quiet, giving all to the stolid authority of Frobish.

"What woman says is we decide where to go," Sonok said. "Depends, so the die is tossed, on whether we like the Earth we would meet.

"You would like my Earth," Frobish said.

"There's no guarantee it'll be your Earth. You have to take that into account."

"You aren't making sense." Frobish shook his head. "My decision is made, nonetheless. We will try to return."

I shrugged. "Try as best you can." We would face the truth later.

"I'll have the Sinieux watch over the machines after I initiate instructions," Frobish said. "Then I would like

Francis to come with me to look at the animal I killed."
I agreed without thinking about his motives. He gave
the metaserpents their orders and pulled down a panel
cover to reveal a small board designed for human
hands. When he was through programming the computers, he continued his instructions to the Sinieux.
His rapport with the animals was perfect—the interaction of an engineer with his tool. There was no
thought of discord or second opinions. The snakes, to
all intents and purposes, were machines keyed only to
his voice. I wondered how far the obedience of his
wives extended.

"Mouse will find food for the bear, and Alouette
will stand guard with the *fusil. Comprens?*" The
woman nodded, and Alouette plucked a rifle from the
hideaway. "When we return, we will all eat."

"I will wait to eat with you," Sonok said, standing
near me.

Frobish looked the bear over coldly. "We do not eat
with tectoes," he said, haughty as a British officer ad-
dressing his servant. "But you will eat the same food
we do."

Sonok stretched out his arms and made two shivers
of anger. "I have never been treated less than a man,"
he said. "I will eat with all or not eat." He looked up at
me with his small golden eyes and asked in Russian,
"Will you go along with him?"

"We don't have much choice," I answered haltingly
in kind.

"What do you recommend?"

"Play along for the moment. I understand." I was

unable to read his expression behind the black mask and white markings; but if I'd been he, I'd have questioned the understanding. This was no time, however, to instruct the bear in assertion.

Frobish opened the hatch to the wrecked room and let me step in first. He then closed the hatch and sealed it. "I've seen the body already," I said. 'What do you want to know?"

"I want your advice on this room," he said. I didn't believe that for an instant. I bent down to examine the creature between the chairs more carefully.

"What did it try to do to you?" I asked.

"It came at me. I thought it was a demon. I shot at it, and it died."

"What caused the rest of this damage?"

"I fired a good many rounds," he said. "I was more frightened then. I'm calm now."

"Thank God for that," I said. "This—he or she—might have been able to help us."

"Looks like a dog," Frobish said. "Dogs cannot help."

For me, that crossed the line. "Listen," I said tightly, standing away from the body. "I don't think you're in touch with what's going on here. If you don't get in touch soon, you might get us all killed. I'm not about to let myself die because of one man's stupidity."

Frobish's eyes widened. "Women do not address men thus," he said.

"This woman does, friend! I don't know what kind of screwy social order you have in your world, but you had damn well better get used to interacting with different sexes, not to mention different species! If you don't, you're asking to end up like this poor thing. It didn't have a chance to say friend or foe, yea or nay! You shot it out of panic, and we can't have any more of that!" I was trembling.

Frobish smiled over grinding teeth and turned to walk away. He was fighting to control himself. I wondered if my own brains were in the right place. The few aspects of this man that were familiar to me couldn't begin to give complete understanding. I was clearly out of my depth, and kicking to stay afloat might hasten death, not slow it.

Frobish stood by the hatch, breathing deeply. "What is the dog-creature? What is this room?"

I turned back to the body and pulled it by one leg from between the chairs. "It was probably intelligent," I said. "That's about all I can tell. It doesn't have any personal effects." The gore was getting to me, and I turned away for a moment. I was tired—oh, so tired I could feel the weary rivers dredging through my limbs. My head hurt abominably. "I'm not an engineer," I said. "I can't tell if any of this equipment is useful to us, or even if it's salvageable. Care to give an opinion?"

Frobish glanced over the room with a slight inclination of one eyebrow. "Nothing of use here."

"Are you sure?"

"I am sure." He looked across the room and sniffed the air. "Too much burned and shorted. You know, there is much that is dangerous here."

"Yes," I said, leaning against the back of a seat.

"You will need protection.

"Oh."

"There is no protection like the bonds of family. You are argumentative, but my wives can teach you our ways. With bonds of family, there will be no uncertainty. We will return, and all will be well."

He caught me by surprise, and I wasn't fast on the uptake. "What do you mean, bonds of family?"

"I will take you to wife and protect you as husband."

"I think I can protect myself, thank you."

"It doesn't seem wise to refuse. Left alone, you will probably be killed by such as this." He pointed at the canine.

"We'll have to get along whether we're family or not. That shouldn't be too hard to understand. And I don't have any inclination to sell myself for security."

"I do not pay money for women!" Frobish said. "Again you ridicule me."

He sounded like a disappointed little boy. I wondered what his wives would think, seeing him butt his head against a wall without sense or sensibility.

"We've got to dispose of the body before it decays," I said. "Help me carry it out of here."

"It isn't fit to touch."

My tiredness took over, and my rationality departed. "You goddamned idiot! Pull your nose down and look at what's going on around you! We're in serious trouble—"

"It isn't the place of a woman to speak thus, I've told you," he said. He approached and raised his hand palm-high to strike. I instinctively lowered my head and pushed a fist into his abdomen. The slap fell like a kitten's paw, and he went over, glancing off my shoulder and twisting my arm into a painful muscle kink. I cursed and rubbed the spot, then sat down on the deck to consider what had happened.

I'd never had much experience with sexism in human cultures. It was disgusting and hard to accept, but some small voice in the back of my mind told me it was no more blameworthy than any other social altitude. His wives appeared to go along with it. At any rate, the situation was now completely shot to hell. There was little I could do except drag him back to his wives and try to straighten things out when he came to. I took him by both hands and pulled him up to the hatch. I unsealed it, then swung him around to take him by the shoulders. I almost retched when one of his shoulders broke the crust on a drying pool of blood and smeared red along the deck.

I miss Jaghit Singh more than I can admit. I think about him and wonder what he'd do in this situation. He is a short, dark man with perfect features and eyes like those in the pictures of Krishna. We formally broke off our relationship three weeks ago, at my behest, for I couldn't see any future in it. He would probably know how to handle Frobish, with a smile and even a spirit of comradeship, but without contradicting his own beliefs. He could make a girl's childhood splinters go back to form the whole log again. He could make these beasts and distortions come together again. Jaghit! Are you anywhere that has seasons? Is it still winter for you? You never did understand the little girl who wanted to play in the snow. Your blood is far too hot and regular to stand up to my moments of indecisive coldness, and you could not—would not—force me to change. I was caught between child and my thirty-year-old form, between spring and winter. Is it spring for you now?

Alouette and Mouse took their husband away from me fiercely, spitting with rage. They weren't talking clearly, but what they shouted in quasi-French made it clear who was to blame. I told Sonok what had happened, and he looked very somber indeed. "Maybe he'll shoot us when he wakes up," he suggested.

To avoid that circumstance, I appropriated the rifle and took it back to my half-room. There was a cabinet intact, and I still had the key. I didn't lock the rifle in, however; better simply to hide it and have easy access to it when needed. It was time to be diplomatic, though all I really wanted for the moment was blessed sleep. My shoulder stung like hell, and the muscles refused to get themselves straight.

When I returned, with Sonok walking point a few steps ahead, Frobish was conscious and sitting in a cot pulled from a panel near the hole. His wives squatted nearby, somber as they ate from metal dishes.

Frobish refused to look me in the eye. Alouette and Mouse weren't in the least reluctant, however, and their gazes threw sparks. They'd be good in a fight, if it ever came down to that. I hoped I wasn't their opposite.

"I think it's time we behaved reasonably," I said.

"There is no reason on this ship," Frobish shot back.

"Aye on that," Sonok said, sitting down to a plate left on the floor. He picked at it, then reluctantly ate, his fingers handling the implements with agility.

"If we're at odds, we won't get anything done," I said.

"That is the only thing which stops me from killing you," Frobish said. Mouse bent over to whisper in his ear. "My wife reminds me you must have time to see the logic of our ways." Were the women lucid despite their anger, or was he maneuvering on his own? "There is also the possibility that you are a leader. I'm a leader, and it's difficult for me to face another leader at times. That is why I alone control this ship."

"I'm not a—" I bit my lip. Not too far, too fast. "We've got to work together and forget about being leaders for the moment."

Sonok sighed and put down the plate. "I have no leader," he said. "That part of me did not follow into this scattershot." He leaned on my leg. "Mascots live best when made whole. So I choose Geneva as my other part. I think my English is good enough now for us to understand."

Frobish looked at the bear curiously. "My stomach hurts," he said after a moment. He turned to me. "You do not hit like a woman. A woman strikes for the soft parts, masculine weaknesses. You go for direct points with knowledge. I cannot accept you as the bear does, but if you will reconsider, we should be able to work together."

"Reconsider the family bond?"

He nodded. To me, he was almost as alien as his snakes. I gave up the fight and decided to play for time.

"I'll have to think about it. My upbringing . . . is hard to overcome," I said.

"We will rest," Frobish said.

"And Sonok will guard," I suggested. The bear straightened perceptibly and went to stand by the hatch. For the moment it looked like a truce had been made, but as cots were pulled out of the walls, I picked up a metal bar and hid it in my trousers.

The Sinieux went to their multilevel cages and lay quiet and still as stone. I slipped into the cot and pulled a thin sheet over myself. Sleep came immediately, and delicious lassitude finally unkinked my arm.

I don't know how long the nap lasted, but it was broken sharply by a screech from Sonok. "They're here! They're here!"

I stumbled out of the cot, tangling one leg in a sheet, and came to a stand only after the Indian family was alert and armed. So much, I thought, for hiding the rifle. "What's here?" I asked, still dopey.

Frobish thrust Sonok away from the hatch with a leg and brought the cover around with a quick arm to slam it shut, but not before a black cable was tossed into the room. The hatch jammed on it, and sparks flew. Frobish stood clear and brought his rifle to his shoulder.

Sonok ran to me and clung to my knee. Mouse

opened the cages and let the Sinieux flow onto the
deck. Frobish retreated from the hatch as it shuddered. The Sinieux advanced. I heard voices from the
other side. They sounded human—like children, in
fact.

"Wait a minute," I said. Mouse brought her pistol
up and aimed it at me. I shut up.

The hatch flung open, and hundreds of fine cables
flew into the room, twisting and seeking, wrapping
and binding. They plucked Frobish's rifle from his
hands and surrounded it like a antibodies on a bac-
terium. Mouse fired her pistol wildly and stumbled,
falling into a nest of cables, which jerked and seized.
Alouette was almost to the hole, but her ankles were
caught and she teetered.

Cables ricocheted from the ceiling and grabbed at
the bundles of Sinieux. The snakes fell apart, some
clinging to the cables like insects on a frog's tongue.
More cables shot out to hold them all, except for a
solitary snake that retreated past me. I was bound
rigid and tight, with Sonok strapped to my knee. The
barrage stopped, and a small shadowed figure stood in
the hatch, carrying a machete. It cleared the entrance
of the sticky strands and stepped into the cabin light,
looking around cautiously. Then it waved to companions behind, and five more entered.

They were identical, each just under half a meter in
height—a little shorter than Sonok—and bald and pink
as infants. Their features were delicate and fetal, with
large gray-green eyes and thin, translucent limbs.
Their hands were stubby-fingered and plump as those

on a Rubens baby. They walked into the cabin with long strides, self-assured, nimbly avoiding the cables.

Sonok jerked at a sound in the corridor—a hesitant high-pitched mewing. "With breasts," he mumbled through the cords.

One of the infantoids arranged a ramp over the bottom seal of the hatch. He then stepped aside and clapped to get attention. The others formed a line, pink fannies jutting, and held their hands over their heads as if surrendering. The mewing grew louder. Sonok's trashcan with breasts entered the cabin, twisting this way and that like a deranged, obscene toy. It was cylindrical, with sides tapering to a fringed skirt at the base. Three levels of pink and nippled paps ringed it at equal intervals from top to bottom. A low, flat head surmounted the body, tiny black eyes examining the cabin with quick, nervous jerks. It looked like nothing so much as the Diana of Ephesus, Magna Mater to the Romans.

One of the infantoids announced something in a piping voice, and the Diana shivered to acknowledge. With a glance around, the same infantoid nodded, and all six stood up to the breasts to nurse.

Feeding over, they took positions around the cabin and examined us carefully. The leader spoke to each of us in turn, trying several languages. None matched our own. I strained to loosen the cords around my neck and jaw and asked Sonok to speak a few of the languages he knew. He did as well as he could through his bonds. The leader listened to him with interest, then echoed a few words and turned to the other five. One nodded and advanced. He spoke to the bear in what sounded like Greek. Sonok stuttered for a moment, then replied in halting fragments.

They moved to loosen the bear's cords, looking up at me apprehensively. The combination of Sonok and six children still at breast hit me deep, and I had to suppress a hysteric urge to laugh.

"I think he is saying he knows what has happened," Sonok said. "They've been prepared for it; they knew what to expect. I think that's what they say."

The leader touched palms with his Greek-speaking colleague, then spoke to Sonok in the same tongue. He held out his plump hands and motioned for the bear to do likewise. A third stepped over rows of crystallized cable to loosen Sonok's arms.

Sonok reluctantly held up his hands, and the two touched. The infantoid broke into shrill laughter and rolled on the floor. His mood returned to utmost gravity in a blink, and he stood as tall as he could, looking us over with an angry expression.

"We are in command," he said in Russian. Frobish and his wives cried out in French, complaining about their bonds. "They speak different?" the infantoid asked Sonok. The bear nodded. "Then my brothers will learn their tongues. What does the other big one speak?"

"English," Sonok said.

The infantoid sighed. "Such diversities. I will learn from her." My cords were cut, and I held out my palms. The leader's hands were cold and clammy, making my arm-hairs crawl.

"All right," he said in perfect English. "Let us tell you what's happened, and what we're going to do."

His explanation of the disruption matched mine closely. "The Alternates have done this to us." He pointed to me. "This big one calls them Aighors. We do not dignify them with a name—we're not even sure they are the same. They don't have to be, you know. Whoever has the secret of disruption, in all universes, is our enemy. We are companions now, chosen from a common pool of those who have been disrupted across a century or so. The choosing has been done so that our natures match closely—we are all from one planet. Do you understand this idea of being companions?"

Sonok and I nodded. The Indians made no response at all.

"But we, members of the Nemi, whose mother is Noctilux, we were prepared. We will take control of the aggregate ship and pilot it to a suitable point, from which we can take a perspective and see what universe we're in. Can we expect your cooperation?"

Again the bear and I agreed, and the others were silent.

"Release them all," the infantoid said with a magnanimous sweep of his hands. "Be warned, however— we can restrain you in an instant, and we are not likely to enjoy being attacked again."

The cords went limp and vaporized with some heat discharge and a slight sweet odor. The Diana rolled over the ramp and left the cabin, with the leader and another infantoid following. The four remaining behind watched us closely, not nervous but intent on our every move. Where the guns had been, pools of slag lay on the floor.

"Looks like we've been overruled," I said to Frobish. He didn't seem to hear me.

In a few hours we were told where we would be allowed to go. The area extended to my cabin and the bathroom, which apparently was the only such facility in our reach. The Nemi didn't seem to need bathrooms, but their recognition of our own requirements was heartening. Within an hour after the takeover, the infantoids had swarmed over the controls in the chamber. They brought in bits and pieces of salvaged equipment, which they altered and fitted with extraordinary speed and skill. Before our next meal, taken from stores in the hole, they understood and controlled all the machinery in the cabin.

The leader then explained to us that the aggregate, or "scattershot," as Sonok had called it, was still far from integrated. At least two groups had yet to be brought into the fold. These were the giant blacks in golden armor, and the beings that inhabited the transparent bubble outside the ship. We were warned that leaving the established boundaries would put us in danger.

The sleep period came. The Nemi made certain we were slumbering before they slept, if they slept at all. Sonok lay beside me on the bunk in my room, snucking faint snores and twitching over distant dreams. I stared up into the dark, thinking of the message tank. That was my unrevealed ace. I wanted to get back to it and see what it was capable of telling me. Did it belong to one of the groups we were familiar with, or was it different, perhaps a party in itself?

* * *

I tried to bury my private thoughts—disturbing, intri-
cate thoughts and sleep, but I couldn't. I was dead-
weight now, and I'd never liked the idea of being
useless. Useless things tended to get thrown out. Since
joining the various academies and working my way
up the line, I'd always assumed I could play some role
in any system I was thrust into.

But the infantoids, though tolerant and even understanding, were self-contained. As they said, they'd
been prepared, and they knew what to do. Uncertainty
seemed to cheer them, or at least draw them together.
Of course they were never more than a few meters
away from a very impressive symbol of security—a
walking breast bank.

The Nemi had their Diana, Frobish had his wives,
and Sonok had me. I had no one. My mind went out,
imagined blackness and fields of stars, and perhaps
nowhere the worlds I knew, and quickly snapped
back. My head hurt, and my back muscles were starting to cramp. I had no access to hormone stabilizers,
so I was starting my period. I rolled over, nudging
Sonok into grumbly half-waking, and shut my eyes
and mind to everything, trying to find a peaceful
glade and perhaps Jaghit Singh. But even in sleep all
I found was snow and broken gray trees.

The lights came up slowly, and I was awakened by
Sonok's movements. I rubbed my eyes and got up
from the bunk, standing unsteadily.

In the bathroom Frobish and his wives were going
about their morning ablutions. They looked at me but
said nothing. I could feel a tension but tried to ignore

it. I was irritable, and if I let any part of my feelings out, they might all pour forth—and then where would I be?

I returned to my cabin with Sonok and didn't see Frobish following until he stepped up to the hatchway and looked inside.

"We will not accept the rule of children," he said evenly. "We'll need your help to overcome them."

"Who will replace them?" I asked.

"I will. They've made adjustments to my machines which I and the Sinieux can handle."

"The Sinieux cages are welded shut," I said.

"Will you join us?"

"What could I do? I'm only a woman."

"I will fight, my wives and you will back me up. I need the rifle you took away."

"I don't have it." But he must have seen my eyes go involuntarily to the locker.

"Will you join us?"

"I'm not sure it's wise. In fact, I'm sure it isn't. You just aren't equipped to handle this kind of thing. You're too limited."

"I have endured all sorts of indignities from you. You are a sickness of the first degree. Either you will work with us, or I will cure you now." Sonok bristled, and I noticed the bear's teeth were quite sharp.

I stood and faced him. "You're not a man," I said. "You're a little boy. You haven't got hair on your chest or anything between your legs—just a bluff and a brag."

He pushed me back on the cot with one arm and

squeezed up against the locker, opening it quickly. Sonok sank his teeth into the man's calf, but before I could get into action the rifle was out and his hand was on the trigger. I fended the barrel away from me, and the first shot went into the corridor. It caught a Nemi and removed the top of his head. The blood and sound seemed to drive Frobish into a frenzy. He brought the butt down, trying to hammer Sonok, but the bear leaped aside and the rifle went into the bunk mattress, sending Frobish off balance. I hit his throat with the side of my hand and caved in his windpipe.

Then I took the rifle and watched him choking against the cabin wall. He was unconscious and turning blue before I gritted my teeth and relented. I took him by the neck and found his pipe with my thumbs, then pushed from both sides to flex the blockage outward. He took a breath and slumped.

I looked at the body in the corridor. "This is it," I said quietly. "We've got to get out of here." I slung the rifle and peered around the hatch seal. The noise hadn't brought anyone yet. I motioned to Sonok, and we ran down the corridor, away from the Indian's control room and the infantoids.

"Geneva," Sonok said as we passed an armored hatch. 'Where do we go?" I heard a whirring sound and looked up. The shielded camera above the hatch was watching us, moving behind its thick gray glass like an eye. "I don't know," I said.

A seal had been placed over the flexible valve in the corridor that led to the bubble. We turned at that point and went past the nook where the message tank had been. It was gone, leaving a few anonymous fixtures behind.

An armored hatch had been punched into the wall several yards beyond the alcove, and it was unsealed. That was almost too blatant an invitation, but I had few other choices. They'd mined the ship like termites. The hatch led into a straight corridor without gravitation. I took Sonok by the arm, and we drifted dreamily down. I saw pieces of familiar equipment studding the walls, and I wondered if people from my world were around. It was an idle speculation. The way I felt now, I doubted I could make friends with anyone. I wasn't the type to establish camaraderie under stress. I was the wintry one.

At the end of the corridor, perhaps a hundred meters down, gravitation slowly returned. The hatch there was armored and open. I brought the rifle up and looked around the seal. No one. We stepped through, and I saw the black in his golden suit, fresh as a ghost. I was surprised; he wasn't. My rifle was up and pointed, but his weapon was down. He smiled faintly.

"We are looking for a woman known as Geneva," he said. "Are you she?"

I nodded. He bowed stiffly, armor crinkling, and motioned for me to follow. The room around the corner was unlighted. A port several meters wide, ribbed with steel beams, opened onto the starry dark. The stars were moving, and I guessed the ship was rolling in space. I saw other forms in the shadows, large and bulky, some human, some apparently not. Their breathing made them sound like waiting predators.

A hand took mine, and a shadow towered over me. "This way."

Sonok clung to my calf, and I carried him with each step I took. He didn't make a sound. As I passed from the viewing room, I saw a blue-and-white curve begin at the top of the port and caught an outline of continent. Asia, perhaps. We were already near Earth. The shapes of the continents could remain the same in countless universes, immobile grounds beneath the thin and pliable paint of living things. What was life like in the distant world-lines where even the shapes of the continents had changed?

The next room was also dark, but a candle flame flickered behind curtains. The shadow that had guided me returned to the viewing room and shut the hatch. I heard the breathing of only one besides myself.

I was shaking. Would they do this to us one at a time? Yes, of course; there was too little food. Too little air. Not enough of anything on this tiny scattershot. Poor Sonok, by his attachment, would go before his proper moment.

The breathing came from a woman, somewhere to my right. I turned to face in her general direction. She sighed. She sounded very old, with labored breath and a kind of pant after each intake.

I heard a dry crack of adhered skin separating, dry lips parting to speak, then the tiny *click* of eyelids blinking. The candle flame wobbled in a current of air. As my eyes adjusted, I could see that the curtains formed a translucent cubicle in the dark.

"Hello," the woman said. I answered weakly. "Is your name Francis Geneva?"

I nodded, then, in case she couldn't see me, and said, "I am."

"I am Junipero," she said, aspirating the j as in Spanish. "I was commander of the High-space ship *Callimachus*. Were you a commander on your ship?"

"No," I replied. "I was part of the crew."

"What did you do?"

I told her in a spare sentence or two, pausing to cough. My throat was like parchment.

"Do you mind stepping closer? I can't see you very well."

I walked forward a few steps.

"There is not much from your ship in the way of computers or stored memory," she said. I could barely make out her face as she bent forward, squinting to examine me. "But we have learned to speak your language from those parts that accompanied the Indian. It is not too different from a language in our past, but none of us spoke it until now. The rest of you did well. A surprising number of you could communicate, which was fortunate. And the little children who suckle—the Nemi—they always know how to get along. We've had several groups of them on our voyages."

"May I ask what you want?"

"You might not understand until I explain. I have been through the mutata several hundred times. You

call it disruption. But we haven't found our home yet,
I and my crew. The crew must keep trying, but I won't
last much longer. I'm at least two thousand years old,
and I can't search forever."

"Why don't the others look old?"

"My crew? They don't lead. Only the top must
crumble away to keep the group flexible, only those
who lead. You'll grow old, too. But not the crew.
They'll keep searching."

"What do you mean, me?"

"Do you know what 'Geneva' means, dear sister?"

I shook my head, no.

"It means the same thing as my name, Junipero.
It's a tree that gives berries. The one who came before
me, her name was Jenevr, and she lived twice as long
as I, four thousand years. When she came, the ship
was much smaller than it is now."

"And your men—the ones in armor—"

"They are part of my crew. There are women, too."

"They've been doing this for six thousand years?"

"Longer," she said. "It's much easier to be a leader
and die, I think. But their wills are strong. Look in the
tank, Geneva."

A light came on behind the cubicle, and I saw the
message tank. The murky fluid moved with a contin-
uous swirling flow. The old woman stepped from the
cubicle and stood beside me in front of the tank. She
held out her finger and wrote something on the glass,
which I couldn't make out.

The tank's creatures formed two images, one of me
and one of her. She was dressed in a simple brown
robe, her peppery black hair cropped into short curls.

She touched the glass again, and her image changed. The hair lengthened, forming a broad globe around her head. The wrinkles smoothed. The body became slimmer and more muscular, and a smile came to the lips. Then the image was stable.

Except for the hair, it was me.

I took a deep breath. "Every time you've gone through a disruption, has the ship picked up more passengers?"

"Sometimes," she said. "We always lose a few, and every now and then we gain a large number. For the last few centuries our size has been stable, but in time we'll probably start to grow. We aren't anywhere near the total yet. When that comes, we might be twice as big as we are now. Then we'll have had, at one time or another, every scrap of ship, and every person who ever went through a disruption."

"How big is the ship now?"

"Four hundred kilometers across. Built rather like a volvox, if you know what that is."

"How do you keep from going back yourself?"

"We have special equipment to keep us from separating. When we started out, we thought it would shield us from a mutata, but it didn't. This is all it can do for us now: it can keep us in one piece each time we jump. But not the entire ship."

I began to understand. The huge bulk of ship I had seen from the window was real. I had never left the grab bag. I was in it now, riding the aggregate, a tiny particle attracted out of solution to the colloidal mass.

Junipero touched the tank, and it returned to its random flow. "It's a constant shuttle run. Each time we return to the Earth to see who, if any, can find their home there. Then we seek out the ones who have the disrupters, and they attack us—send us away again."

"Out there—is that my world?"

The old woman shook her head. "No, but it's home to one group—three of them. The three creatures in the bubble."

I giggled. "I thought there were a lot more than that."

"Only three. You'll learn to see things more accurately as time passes. Maybe you'll be the one to bring us all home."

"What if I find my home first?"

"Then you'll go, and if there's no one to replace you, one of the crew will command until another comes along. But someone always comes along, eventually. I sometimes think we're being played with, never finding our home, but always having a Juniper to command us." She smiled wistfully. "The game isn't all bitterness and bad tosses, though. You'll see more things, and do more, and be more, than any normal woman."

"I've never been normal," I said.

"All the better."

"If I accept."

"You have that choice."

"'Junipero,'" I breathed. "Geneva." Then I laughed. "How do you choose?"

The small child, seeing the destruction of its thousand companions with each morning light and the skepticism of the older ones, becomes frightened and wonders if she will go the same way. Someone will raise the shutters and a sunbeam will impale her and she'll phantomize. Or they'll tell her they don't believe she's real. So she sits in the dark, shaking. The dark becomes fearful. But soon each day becomes a triumph. The ghosts vanish, but she doesn't, so she forgets the shadows and thinks only of the day. Then she grows older, and the companions are left only in whims and background thoughts. Soon she is whittled away to nothing; her husbands are past, her loves are firm and not potential, and her history stretches away behind her like carvings in crystal. She becomes wrinkled, and soon the daylight haunts her again. Not every day will be a triumph. Soon there will be a final beam of light, slowly piercing her jellied eye, and she'll join the phantoms.

But not now. Somewhere, far away, but not here. All around, the ghosts have been resurrected for her to see and lead. And she'll be resurrected, too, always under the shadow of the tree name.

"I think," I said, "that it will be marvelous."

So it was, thirty centuries ago. Sonok is gone, two hundred years past; some of the others have died, too, or gone to their own Earths. The ship is five hundred kilometers across and growing. You haven't come to replace me yet, but I'm dying, and I leave this behind to guide you, along with the instructions handed down by those before me.

Your name might be Jennifer, or Ginepra, or something else, but you will always be me. Be happy for all of us, darling. We will be forever whole.

Greg Bear Guest of Honor
Millennium Philcon
59th World Science
Convention–2001

Transcribed by Edie Stern
Edited by Greg Bear

It's a true privilege of course, everyone knows that, to be Guest of Honor at a Worldcon. It's one of the premium honors afforded people from the fan community and the convention runners, who are really to be blessed here so let's give a hand for the people that do the hard work. The people behind the scenes, all the people doing the paper work, all the people listening to writers and guests complaining madly about things not being right, and then making them go right. That's an extremely tough job.

It's kind of daunting to stand up here and deliver a guest of honor speech at Worldcon; you have to sum up your entire life and leave them inspired at the end and get it all done in one speech and so I'm not really going to do that. I'm going to talk about a special year. A very strange year. A year that sums up in a lot of ways what I got into science fiction for when I was just a kid eight or nine years old. Didn't really even know what I wanted to do. The year is 2001. It's a magic year. It should have been the year in which we celebrated so many tremendous things and, in fact, we have been celebrating tremendous things.

On the personal side, this has been a fascinating year, with many pluses and many highlights, and one very sad moment. Which shouldn't have happened in 2001. I don't know who to blame for this entirely, but I'm going to get into that.

Quite often when I give talks at conventions, I talk about what science fiction did for me, the paying forward of all the writers who talk to young people, who encourage them, who basically give them the secret words and the secret handshakes and let them move up and become writers themselves. There's no way to pay back the writers who inspired us, so we simply pay it forward and that is how conventions like this remain so incredibly friendly and accessible and where there is outreach, incredible outreach to everybody, and acceptance that would make any democratic society either extremely proud or extremely suspicious, I'm not sure which.

Anyway, I just wanted to tell all of you out there, all of you since the beginning of science fiction conventions, you have *kicked ass*! For American culture, for American literature, for young people everywhere who come into conventions and meet people who are due to inspire them. You have changed the world, and you've changed my life.

For me, this began in a real sense back in 1968 in Baycon. I guess there's a panel (is there a panel?) coming up on Baycon. If I can I'll make it there, but if I'm cross scheduled it won't work.

Baycon: I was 16 years old. I rode on the bus to Berkeley with two friends, David Clark and Scott Shaw, and we were all very young and we stayed at the Shattuck Hotel, and somehow or other managed to get to the Claremont Hotel and to hang out with people, and it was mind blowing. You could walk through the lobby of the Claremont Hotel and there would be, oh, Lin Carter, sitting over here on a circular couch holding forth. You walked over here, and there was John W. Campbell and his wife sitting behind a table. You step into the ice cream shop and there's Ray Bradbury, whom we had already met and established a friendship with, holding forth. And then, as all of us kids were sitting there, watching, talking to Ray in very friendly and open terms, in walks John Brunner and he's carrying a copy of his new book, and he gives it to Ray, and we're all watching, awestruck, and Ray says "Oh, thank you John" and it's *Stand on Zanzibar.* And we walk down the hallway, and there's Dorothy Fontana, and they're showing *Star Trek* episodes, and handing out free copies of a Ballantine paperback book on *Star Trek*, and we're glum. We're sitting out on the concrete at the front doorway, you know, teenagers being glum the way we can, because we didn't get copies, and Dorothy walks out and she says "Why are you so sad?"

"We didn't get one."

To which Dorothy says, "I'd give you this one, but it's my only copy."

Dorothy Fontana, of course, was one of the people, who along with Gene Roddenberry, and David Gerrold and a number of other writers, established the look and feel and sound of the television show that changed fandom forever. After *Star Trek*, suddenly women started appearing at conventions. They appeared at Baycon; they came out in droves.

We had the SCA, we had costuming, filking, Edgar Rice Burroughs fandom, pulp fandom, movie fandom, characterized most succinctly by my friends the Warrens, Bill and Beverly; we had all these ways in which fandom spread out to conquer the earth and a lot of people thought this was the splintering of fandom; the focus taken away. What they had forgotten is that before costuming and the SCA there were also the poker players who never read science fiction, people who collected *Argosy* magazine, and went to the conventions just for that. There's always been a fragmentation of interests.

What we were doing was creating explorers

who would go out and infiltrate and shape the entire culture of the world and 1968 was really the first I think, possibly 67–68, the first years in which that became patently obvious. That we were going to win. That we had the best and the brightest, from Ray Bradbury already world famous, to John Brunner, who was writing incredible books that to this day are groundbreaking, like *Stand on Zanzibar* and *The Sheep Look Up*, to guest of honor Philip Jose Farmer, already involved in his Riverworld series. To John W. Campbell, whose quiet steady influence at that point was being kind of derided, and yet Campbell was one of the fathers. You could still go back and touch one of the fathers of modern science fiction. Almost as great in its way as going back and meeting H. G. Wells would have been. Pretty incredible convention.

1968.

I was 16 years old.

I had some paintings hanging in the art show room. I had been working on paintings; I'd discovered acrylics and later found out about oils, and I had painted some of these things. They were pretty crude, but they weren't terrible, and they were hanging in the art show. And Bjo Trimble walks up to me and asks if I'd like to do some more art for her publications. Bjo Trimble was at this time the secret mother of fandom, for me anyway, and eventually she sent me a set of clippings of *Star Trek* episodes. Actual 35 mm film clips which had strange little things like people breaking up laughing and so on. They weren't usable—they were outtakes. They were bloopers and special effect shots and I picked things out of those stacks of film clips and stared at them in the sunlight, and drew pictures of them for Bjo's *Star Trek Concordance* and other publications, and started realizing there was a thing called fandom. And that you could send sketches and pen and ink illustrations to fanzines in Los Angeles, *Shangri L'Affaires*, and magazines like that. I got one of my first illustrations published in the *Shangri L'Affaires Christmas Calendar*. It was happy go lucky Yog Sothoth wishing you a happy Christmas, a merry Christmas. We remember these things, because when we're young these things are as important as anything that happens later, and Science Fiction gets us when we're young. Science fiction fandom taught me what it was like to have my name in print.

Science fiction touches us deeply, it tells its that life is an endless adventure. It also tells us that along the way there will be more than adventure; there will be trauma, and sadness and tragedy and misery, and that nevertheless, pointless or no, depending on your philosophy, and we absorb all in the sf community, science fiction reminds us that life is an adventure, and that change is an adventure. How can we quantify *that* in a world that seemed perpetually locked in teenage angst about fashion and class and social standing. How can we qualify the quality of this vision that is passed on to children through the mesh of *Star Trek*, through *Star Wars*, through the seventy thousand science fiction shows on television we can't possibly keep up with, many of which are very fine in individual episodes if not in the whole. This total mass vision that tells us that life is an adventure, that exploration is necessary. That what we do and what we think matters in the universe. When we are not concerned about our social status or bank accounts, we all become fans. We become enthusiasts and there is nothing that the jaded journalists and historians of the world love less than enthusiasts. We are supposed to be sophisticated. We are supposed to be knowing and untouched, and we are supposed to be cool. Very few fans are cool. (laughter) Well, Robert Silverberg is cool, but I've seen him be uncool. (laughter) And when I look deep into Robert's beautiful eyes, I know that in his heart he is really uncool. (crowd laughter)

Most of us in this room are caught in a perpetual and wonderfully regal childhood where we can go back and touch those things that touched us early—the comic books, the pulp magazines, the old stories that were honored this evening in this lovely ceremony, the Retro Hugos. You don't see Retro Nobels. You don't see the literary brahmans going back and handing Nobels out to Nikos Kazantzakis and James Joyce or to Jorge Luis Borges. You don't see them handing out what they should have handed out. You don't see that. We do that. We look backwards because we know how to look forwards. We know how to accept change and to revere those who changed us. (Applause)

And I mean here, I do mean a friendly reverence. We are not frightened of our saints. We are not frightened of our gods and our mentors. Because they helped teach us the ropes. They weren't mysterious and lofty and inscrutable. They were people. They were editors. They were people having troubles. They were people writing books or not writing books. They were people acting drunk in the hallway. They were people behaving—pontificating—sometimes wisely, sometimes not. They were people, they were people everywhere we looked. Wonderful people blessed with wonderful visions, or nightmares, or both.

One of those was a man I first saw in 1966 in the 20 minutes that I spent at the Westercon in San Diego, California, at the Stardust Hotel which shall remain *Bouncing Potatoes* forever. Famous for its disappointed hookers, and for the committee that was called up to service in the navy. I was only there for 20 minutes. I had read about it in the local newspaper. I was 14 years old and the only face I recognized was, god bless him, Forrest J Ackerman. I read *Famous Monsters* and *Space-*

man. Even then I preferred *Spaceman* to *Famous Monsters*, but I now realize *Famous Monsters* was cool too. And Forry was sitting in the lobby of the Stardust Hotel, perfectly willing to talk to a 14 year old kid who had just wandered in, sitting down, talking about science fiction for 20 minutes. I didn't know you could stay. Didn't know that.

My parents found all this to be vaguely interesting. They found the sweaty dealers handing out pulp magazines in the small, very small, dealers room to be a little strange, but they accepted it. They didn't discourage me. My parents, of course, are the ones I have to thank chiefly for all of this, they were excellent parents, and I had so many other parents as well. Some of them to this day might not know it. You can't pay back, really, because a lot of these people are too modest. You must pay forward.

This gentleman that I saw, but did not speak to, would have been a little over 6 feet tall. Big shock of hair. A bright expression, a friendly expression. He could look at you with his blue eyes and you'd know instantly this was someone you could talk to. He was a writer; he was a very good writer. In 1959, I think it was, he had been the youngest Guest of Honor at a world science fiction convention. Started writing in 1947. His name was Poul Anderson, and already to me he was a legend.

I first really met Poul, to speak to, for him to

recognize me, in 1970 and 1971. I was writing pretty furiously then, but publishing almost nothing. Didn't matter. I could chat with these writers, hang out, get to meet them, and so gradually Poul came into my view. Astrid came into my view too. (laughter). And that was very nice also. And as the years passed by, more and more conventions, more and more discussions, sitting down and talking about black holes with Poul and a number of other people at one convention, you know, regaling pretty young women about naked singularities and all, hanging out with Poul and Karen and watching how they interacted with fans and with each other.

This was the man who had written *The High Crusade*, and for me, two seminal works I had read back to back, *The Broken Sword* and *Tau Zero*, in 1970 and 1971, I'd read those, and I'd realized that was the range that you could have in one human being. You could do Norse tragedy, tell of strange Wagnerian, Scandinavian elves at the same time that you could tell us that we could live forever and survive the end of time in a spaceship based on physics, not magic. What an amazing range. And I think at that point, I realized that I might never have that range, but by god it would be worthwhile to try. If Poul could do it, because Poul looked so modest and unassuming, maybe I could do it too. So I set out to do that.

I loved fantasy. I loved H. P. Lovecraft and

Clark Ashton Smith and Ray Bradbury and I loved Theodore Sturgeon and I also loved John W. Campbell and Robert Heinlein and Isaac Asimov and Arthur C. Clarke. And especially Arthur C. Clarke. It was like I was constantly swinging back between the two extremes of Arthur C. Clarke and Ray Bradbury, and along the way meeting Poul going both directions, (laughter) and actually being able to hang out with most of these people, to meet them.

In the early 1980s I attended an ABA with my wife, Astrid, and walked across the street beside Robert and Ginnie Heinlein. Mr. Heinlein looked at me, nodded his head, and said, "Pretty good book you wrote there." I'm baffled, wondering "what, who, who, where," you know. Total disbelief that Robert Heinlein himself would read my novel. I believe he was referring to *Strength of Stones*, just published by Ace.

Poul did the same thing to me in 1976 after I had a cover story in *Analog*, and the same reaction—you know, "you're talking to me?" I couldn't really believe that the writers who had inspired me were reading and enjoying what I was writing.

My god. Is that possible? I still don't believe it. I come here, and you see me wandering with a camera on my chest because this is a great chance to get pictures of my favorite writers. (laughter) Sorry guys—I'm still a kid. (applause)

It's easy to be self-important and arrogant, and

I have that problem in spades, as Astrid will tell you. But I'll remind you, I'll tell you all, whether you were there or not, fandom raised me, you raised me. All of you. This is a culture.

As I've said before, and I'll continue to say because it is true, this is the most important literary movement, artistic movement, in western literature and western arts and popular culture since the Romantics. And we've lasted and stayed viable decades longer. We are the heirs to the Romantics, but we've carved our own ground. We're the American literary equivalent of jazz, and we dance and we sing and we tap in a way that few can imitate successfully. And our success is something that no one really acknowledges outside of our field, but it's a success that has taught tens of millions, hundreds of millions of people, in the last thirty years, around the world, what a robot is, what warp drive is, what a starship is, what a ray gun is, what a blaster is, what artificial intelligence is, what a clone is, a hobbit, dungeons, dragons, Conan, what all of these things are. What matter transporters are.

In 1968 when I finished my last year in high school, there were maybe one out of ten kids who could have told you what those things were. Now, its ten out of ten. This is worse than Marxism (laughter and applause). The communists are gone but fandom lives on. (more laughter and applause)

When I married Astrid, Poul didn't sit down and

lecture me. He didn't sit down and lecture her. I became part of the family. I'd come to dinners and we'd just sit and talk and it always felt odd and wonderful to me. That here was a guy that I could just talk to as a guy, as a friend, but he was the same man who had helped raise me when I was 13, 14, 15, 16 years old reading the *High Crusade* and reading stories in *Analog* for which he got these beautiful covers by John Schoenherr and Chesley Bonestell. The writer who had a career that I could only dream of was my friend, and we often loosely touched on collaborating, but you know, we never did. I'm not much of a collaborator. Poul has collaborated with many people, including one of his best friends, Gordy Dickson. Gordy is gone this year too.

2001—a strange year. I regularly send e-mail to Sir Arthur C. Clarke. Given the weight of messages he receives in this year of years, it's a wonder he can respond, but he does. A mutual friend, Karl Anders, visited Sri Lanka and took a couple of photographs that are posted on the con's web site which I think perfectly exemplify the spirit of science fiction. Karl took some of my books to Sir Arthur when he went to Sri Lanka, and snapped pictures of Arthur holding the books on his lap as he's sitting comfortably in his wheelchair, and then Arthur said "Let's show Greg what we really think about his works." and the second photo has Arthur holding up a book and (gestures holding his nose). Look that up on the convention web site. That's being blessed, isn't it? I mean, when you can crack jokes with people like that, or when I can drive down or fly down to Los Angeles, and call up Ray Bradbury and say "Ray, I'm coming to town; can we go out and have lunch?" and he says "Sure," And we get together and we talk like kids . . . We talk like kids. And Ray tells me about the movies that he's making, about the movies that are disappointing him or turning out wonderfully. And I'm saying to myself, "Man, I wish I could talk about any movies at all." It's just his life. He's being perfectly open with me. I've always loved Ray Bradbury. We've been friends for thirty-three years.

I first met Ray Bradbury in 1968. The two points between which my pendulum swings, Arthur C. Clarke and Ray Bradbury, and I met both of them for the first time in 1968.

The same love applied to many different authors snuck up on me with Poul. Poul was quiet. He was charming. He never offended; he never yelled. Some people said he didn't suffer fools gladly, but you know, he suffered a lot of fools. He suffered me. And he got under my skin. It was as if he would always be available to talk to. These writers that I met seemed to be able to live forever, and some of them probably will. Jack Williamson for example. They're our history. They did so many incredible things and pumped so many incredible ideas and philosophies into our culture that to watch them pass has always shaken me.

When John Brunner died at a convention, he stole one of the ideas I wanted to turn into a mainstream novel. About a writer who realizes that his home always was science fiction conventions—that he had to go back there to die. But John didn't plan this, he didn't go there intentionally. It crept up on him. Suddenly he was gone. Other writers passing over the years. I can't go through the list for this year because it's just been dreadful.

Some of them have led long and full lives, but Poul did not live long enough. I blame the Norns for this. I really do. They screwed up. Here's a man who helped make the 21st century. He should have lived longer to see what he had done.

Why?

Selfishly, we would say out there in the audience, you would say, "It's because we could get more great books out of him." *Mother of Kings* is a wonderful novel; it's like going back to the young Poul Anderson of the 1950s and reading *The Broken Sword* all over again. It's startling. It's like Sibelius put on paper. It's a startlingly fresh and young book. Poul did not get old in his writing. He did not get crotchety and cranky. He was always the same varied, smooth, unassuming stylist. He didn't get old. Now isn't that a model? It's the model that I learned as well from nearly every other science fiction writer. From Ray Bradbury, who told us constantly that we always remain teenagers, and those who don't say that they are teenagers in their inner brain are lying. Some people I found out later really do get old, and I feel sorry for them. Poul didn't. Poul didn't really change. He got under my skin. I thought he was going to be there forever. That we'd always be able to get together and have dinners and talk and then Poul and Karen could come up to visit, or we could fly down to the Bay area.

The last time I saw Poul I flew down to Orinda, rented a car, drove out to the house in the afternoon. Karen had laid out a gorgeous lunch and we sat under the tree—the inside of their tiny house was too hot that day—and we chatted for about three hours. And then I had to leave. Poul checked into the hospital for tests not long after. Weeks passed, and the news got worse.

And it was a phone call, or a couple of phone calls and Astrid had to fly down there and all of a sudden he was gone.

It is as if a huge silence fell over us. I'll tell you one thing. He touched us all. He was mainstream in our hearts and minds.

The work of all of these authors is part of American flesh and bone now. We have won. We have won an incredible cultural war to tell people that the future is important. That you must be there to criticize and yell and stomp and scream and enthuse and be alive. That you have to live the future before you can make it. You have to imagine it and dream it. And Poul did that for us. In a quiet way he punched his way through. He was one of the strongest science fiction writers that we have had. And he did it so quietly. And it embarrasses me to say I am not like that. I am more arrogant and more headstrong and more forward, and most of my friends, the Killer B's, are the same way.

And Poul is still the quiet and unassuming voice of science fiction welcoming us all. How many conventions have you been to where Poul and Karen were there, friendly, accessible, greeting, not self important, not neurotic about their presence, about their established place in the field. So many of the science fiction writers were and are like this. And you must understand how different this is from other areas of literature where you have to fight and scratch and claw and biff people in drunken rages to get a reputation and get reviewed by the *New York Times*, where you must argue in print with the people who are most like you and all the people out there watch this much as they watch American sports or politics and they kind of feel cynical and cheapened by the whole thing.

You don't see that much in science fiction. You see a little bit of it. Just enough to keep us, you know, gossiping. (laugh) We have our sacred monsters, too. And some of them are quite wonderful sacred monsters. You know the people we always want to talk about, and if they run you ragged and curse you, you feel strangely blessed. That's more like the literary experience of New York. Some of us have tried, perhaps too hard, to suck up to New York literary culture, to offer up our saints and our offspring, crying out, look here, we are worthy. We don't need to worry about that. We've won.

Poul was not like that. Most of the writers I've met weren't really like that. All the writers stand out as individuals, as distinctive personalities, but in the long run, our differences don't matter because we are all part of the same tissue and the same flesh and we have many of the same goals. And I'm not sure we as science fiction writers are even quite aware of what those goals are. All we want to do, we say over and over again, is tell stories that raise the hair on the back of your neck, or make you laugh, or make you wonder. It seems like the rest of the world out there in the twentieth century was so traumatized that it lost its sense of wonder and started to feel instead a sense of dread and fear, and the thought of change terrified people, quite rightly. Science fiction fans are naive. We don't always understand that change can mean death and sickness and disease and trauma. We don't get that really. It's not part of our tissue to understand that. The outside world knew that and so it acted as a kind of foil while we grew up. It ignored us in the 30s, the 40s, the 50s. It ignored us and despised us and when it met with us it didn't understand what we were talking about and that was great because we could grow in the womb unbothered, being ignored, developing our own tropes and our own fashions and our own ideas, and suddenly when we were born, perhaps in the 1960s, and spread out everywhere, we found that people like Robert Heinlein had gone before and Isaac Asimov and Arthur C. Clarke and Harlan Ellison and Gene Roddenberry had gone before and Ray Bradbury had gone before and sown the ground with thousands and thousands of infants springing up to read the books, to watch the movies, to make the movies, to write the books.

Poul Anderson was there. He did it quietly. He wrote almost up to the end. The room in Orinda where he wrote for over 40 years I last saw a month ago. Snapped pictures of it. Couldn't believe he wasn't there. The bed had been taken out. He died in that room, where he had written most of his books and stories. The photographs of his grandchildren, my son and daughter, Erik and Alexandra, were still on the walls. Some of his artifacts passed on from his grandfather, his grandmother, pictures of his grandmother, a lot of textbooks, a lot of research materials, beautifully printed and illustrated sagas in Danish, history books, science books, well-thumbed reference books like Dole's *Habitable Planets for Man*, and his own books sitting in shelves under the window, with a huge broadsword hanging nearby. Being in that room was like looking into the heart of Poul Anderson. It was a very pleasant, small study, out of which sprang starships and aliens and elves.

When I wrote my own books, the fantasy novels, *The Infinity Concerto* and *The Serpent Mage*, I borrowed Poul's elves. He taught me what elves really were. I borrowed them, and some people came back later and said to me these elves weren't like other fantasy elves, they were more like aliens, and I said to myself, "But isn't that the way elves would really be? Aren't elves inscrutable and powerful beings that should scare the pants off you if they meet you in the dark?" Really, I think they are. Poul taught me that. Poul influenced me in that way and so many others.

Poul influenced me when I wrote my hard science fiction. I wanted to make a movie out of *Tau Zero*. In 1977, when I turned in a piece for the *Los Angeles Times* calendar section on this movie that was coming out, that had come out, that had really done very well at the box office, I wrote a short article explaining some of the possible predecessors and inspirations for new film, *Star Wars*, everything from Jack Williamson to Doc Smith to Robert Heinlein and Asimov, and suddenly I started getting phone calls from studios, and they wanted me to come in and explain why they had rejected *Star Wars*. (laughter)

I heard the rumor that the people at Universal Studios, the story editors, who had taken meetings with George Lucas and had rejected his proposal, had all been fired. And so, Dino de Laurentiis Productions wanted me to explain to them why they hadn't bought *Star Wars*. I couldn't explain that to them.

But then they said, "Can you tell us what other movie we should do?" and I said "How about *Tau Zero*?" So I called up Poul, and I said, "Would you let me present this to them?" and Poul, very naively said "Yes, sure." So I took in a proposal to them and just as they had turned down *Star Wars*, they turned down *Tau Zero*. I took in *The House on the Borderland*, by William Hope Hodgson and they didn't like that either and finally in my exasperation, I realized they were just kind of playing with me, just having fun. I was getting fed well in good Beverly Hills restaurants around Rodeo Drive. But I had not come prepared. At 27 years old, I didn't have a screenplay under my arm; I wasn't made for this. And they asked, "What *other* movie would you make from any science fiction novel, if you could make just one?"

And I said, "You know, I think Alexander Jodorowski has let *Dune* go. I think it's available now." So they made *Dune*. (laughter)

Now Brian (Herbert) tells me they'd actually bought the book before that, but I haven't established this to my complete (satisfaction)—they didn't say they'd bought it. They didn't say "oh we already own the rights to that." Maybe I was just confirming what they'd already done, but you know that was pretty interesting. They didn't make any of my books.

Tau Zero is now being taken around Los Angeles. A number of very interesting people really want to do something by Poul. *Brain Wave* is quite popular. *Brain Wave* was Poul's first major novel. It's a Jimmy Stewart movie. It's a Tom Hanks movie. It's a Tim Robbins movie. It's about animals that get smart and dumb people that get smart. It could be a wonderful film. It's Frank Capra meets Steven Spielberg in a lot of ways and yet it's a very convincing novel. It's just gritty and convincing and real and totally sympathetic and in the end, loving. *Brain Wave* could get made, any minute. Who knows? Because many of the people who are in the studios now, many of the people who write the screenplays, and nearly all of the good directors are science fiction fans. They may not come to conventions, because you know when you're worth two or three hundred million dollars you can't just hang out at a convention. You've got places to go and people to see.

You're caught up in the angst of maintaining your career. But when you pierce some of our best filmmakers to their heart and ask, what do you love? What do you want to do? People like James Cameron, and George Lucas and Stanley Kubrick and Steven Spielberg, and we could go on and on. Alex Proyas, I could be leaving people out, Luc Besson, Jan De Bont, Steve Norrington, and all of these people. What they say is "we want to do a good science fiction movie". They say it in many accents, because we've spread our words and ideas all over the planet.

I've had my 21st or 22nd translation. I don't know how many languages Poul was translated into. But it was at least as many as he had Hugos and Nebulas and Gandalfs and everything else out there. He had awards that aren't being given out anymore. The shelf of awards stretched so long a lot of them had to be stored in the garage.

Humility was taught to me as I looked at Poul's shelf of awards, and as my pitiful few were beginning to stack up. And even at the last count, he was beating me out. I don't know how many he had in all.

So I'm going to try to get some of those movies made.

The people I grew up with are now making movies. Fellow science fiction readers and fans are making movies. When I was 16 years old, another young man attending Baycon, whom I had met earlier when I first attended a speech by Ray Bradbury, was Phil Tippett. I wanted to be a stop motion animation fellow like Ray Harryhousen, but Phil showed me his sculptures of dinosaurs made in clay and wax and bronze, and I said forget it. Just forget it.

Over the years, Phil went on to do everything from *Star Wars* to *Jurassic Park* to *Starship Troopers*. He now employs 200 people in his studio in Berkeley. Phil and his wife Jules make so many movies I can't keep up with them.

The science fiction field expands out from the friends of Poul Anderson. Jack Vance for example. Elegant writer. Influential writer. Read by people like Jimmy Hendrix. Who then influenced people like Paul Allen. Whose favorite writer is Jack Vance. Most of the billionaires that we've been fortunate enough to meet in Seattle are science fiction fans. We get invited through Neal Stephenson, and George Dyson to go to Jeff Bezos's house for a party celebrating their finished manuscripts. I look at the book shelves in Mr. Bezos's library and there's a couple of yards of science fiction books.

The politicians read science fiction. Gregory Benford tells me that Harry Truman loved reading pulp science fiction magazines for relaxation. It's in Truman's memoirs.

Many of the scientists at Los Alamos, New Mexico, had subscriptions to *Analog,* or rather to *Astounding* magazine. That's how Cleve Cartmill got in trouble. And you know how he got in trouble? You can read this in Gregory Benford's essay in my collection *New Legends*. "Old Legends" he calls it. They got in trouble because their issues of *Astounding* arrived. There was a story by Cleve Cartmill in there, and they talked about it in the cabin after their long day at work. People like Edward Teller and Feynman. They talked about the science fiction they had read, about this story about nuclear fission, and the FBI agent sitting in the shadows in the corner perked up, and started taking notes and sweating bullets and saying "Oh my god. It's out there. Who let this loose?" And they went and knocked on John W. Campbell's door, and they said "Can you explain this, Mr. Campbell?" And I think he quietly explained it and (I paraphrase, and reconstruct) said "It's been going in science fiction since 1914. *World Set Free*, H. G. Wells. There it is. Go look at it gentlemen. I didn't do this and you want me to stop publishing stories about nuclear fission?" And they said "Oh no no no. Never mind. Never mind." And John W. Campbell had set Cleve Cartmill out as a belled sheep to see if there were any eagles waiting to strike, and when they came back and struck, he said "Ah, they're building an atom bomb." I just *KNOW* he said this. (laughter) He had that kind of mind. (applause)

That means that science fiction has known sin, too. Because both Heisenberg and Leo Szilard when they were faced with this distinct possibility of nuclear fission being used to make a bomb, they said, "I think it will be more like what H. G. Wells wrote in *The World Set Free*." (written in 1913 and 1914, just on the cusp of the first world war). Wells got it right. He got so many things right. So many of our writers have got things right, but they don't get them exactly right. We're not prophets. We're not here to inform the rich people of the world on how to make more money, or to inform governments on how to direct themselves. We are here to allow you to dream your dreams and make them happen, and have your nightmares a little in advance so you can prevent them from happening.

That's what we do. It's an incredibly powerful function, when you realize that we have gone out and touched the lives of so many people. All of you out here, by contributing to the culture of science fiction fandom, you are, in a very real sense the center of the universe. On this planet. You have done something that historians will be discussing, once they get their act together, for centuries.

Jerry Pournelle had Poul and Gregory Benford and Larry Niven, and a number of us, Dean Ing and a number of other writers, Robert Heinlein (Larry should remind me who the rest of them were). Bjo Trimble was there with her daughter, Lora. Lot of science fiction writers getting together with generals, rocket scientists young and old, new and experienced, and people from NASA, and politicians and discussing this possibility that perhaps nuclear war was going to become a push button affair where computers would make the decision, and no one could tolerate that and we had to start building defensive shields. So we started putting together different ideas, General Danny Graham had one vision and some of the writers had another. And they had a science fiction fan for a president; his name was Ronald Reagan.

Now we laugh. Do you want your presidents to be smart? Do you want them to be dreamers? Or do you want them to be lucky? Because this thing that went forth that Ronald Reagan did was the vastest bluff in the blue bottom baboon history of the whole cold war. Ronald Reagan said we could put a whole umbrella over the United States and protect you, and he said it to Gorbachev, and Gorbachev said, "My God. My god. They're Americans. They may be right." And Gorbachev himself apparently, has indicated this was a major factor in him folding his cards, and going home.

Science fiction writers helped the rocket scientists elucidate their vision, clarified it. They put it together in prose that Ronald Reagan could understand and Ronald Reagan, who read science fiction, said "why not?" and he was lucky and so, that thing that had terrified me as a child, surviving the Cuban missile crisis, that thing that we had all thought would go on into the 21st century, that I had written about continuing into the 21st century, the ever present shadow of nuclear war, all of that, suddenly wasn't really there any more. And in *Terminator 2*, James Cameron had to have one of his characters say, "Well, aren't we friends with the Russians?" We really kind of are. There are so many science fiction readers who are Russians. When Ray Bradbury was in a reception line, waiting to meet Gorbachev and Raisa, when he got up there, Gorbachev looked at his name tag, and the interpreter said his name, and Gorbachev says "RAY BRADBURY!" He says: "Raisa, this is our daughter's favorite author!" And they gave him a big hug, and every time Gorbachev comes into LA, he wants to get together with Ray Bradbury.

Ok. One-ups-manship. Arthur C. Clarke gets to meet the Pope. (laughter) Isaac Asimov got to meet everybody. Newt Gingrich one time, walked into Isaac's New York apartment. Now Isaac was a New York, very liberal Jew, and Newt Gingrich was this guy from Georgia who's about to wreak havoc with the US Congress and President Clinton and everything, but at that point he was a freshman Congressman and he was just in heaven to be in Asimov's apartment. We've got to get more democrats to read science fiction. They tend to read mysteries. And James Bond. That was what Roosevelt and Kennedy liked to read—mysteries and James Bond.

So my politics over the years have been kind of indefinable, because I've been taught from so many different directions, by so many different people, so many different realities and views of how politics works. I watched Jerry Pournelle wangle this thing, along with a lot of other people of course, into a political reality that really did help to shut down the Cold War. I had a very small part in that. I can't claim real credit for it. It wasn't my original vision. But I helped. We all helped. Science fiction fandom helped.

Because we had laid the groundwork for the impressions the Russians got of America that we could do anything. That we could build rockets. We could go to the moon. We could beat them in a moon race, hands down. We couldn't beat them into space first. They were very, very good and they still are. But we inspired the Russians, and Russian science fiction inspired the Russians. And American science fiction finally took over the Russian. Getting to sit down with Doris Lessing and the Strugatsky brothers at Brighton in 1987, I believe it was or 88, was really impressive because Doris Lessing, one of the great writers in the literary circles, was a science fiction fan. She was writing science fiction. The Strugatsky brothers, we would sit there, and discuss whether or not science fiction was really about story telling or in a sense a satire, and trying to bring about change. And they were quite convinced that it was a secret message that would slip past the Politburo and effect change, and they were right, in Russia it did. But American science fiction hit the Politburo hard, as we know now. It hit the nomenclature. They were watching our science fiction movies. We had influence. We, who were not really appreciated by the *New York Times*, changed history. Who's written that story? It's not out there yet. So, in a sense, science fiction has redeemed itself from the sin that it knew when it informed the nuclear scientists back in the 1940s that a bomb could be built. We helped shut down that particular nightmare; it's not completely gone. We can still write scenarios. Tom Clancy still has a career. (laughter)

But for a minute there he was very scared. And so was I. What are we going to write about? What are we going to do next? Ok, we changed the world. There's the ending to the famous novel which was made into a famous movie which I believe goes back to an old fannish saying. I believe it was Claude Degler, who said "We have a cosmic mind. What do we do now?" And of course, the ending of 2001 is really that line rewritten. [Actually, this was a sarcastic response written on a postcard to Degler by Jack Speer.-Joe Siclari] [Jack Speer was at the convention—more continuity!-Greg]

What do we do now? It's the 21st century. It's 2001. It's official, no matter how populist you are. It really is the 21st century. The 20th century is past. Science fiction was essentially made by H. G. Wells, and a fair number of other people in the early years of the 20th century. We must look back of course to Verne, and to Twain, and to all the people who wrote science fiction going back to Mary Shelley. They were seminal. But H. G. Wells was our Shakespeare. He laid down all of the forms.

Why don't we get credit for helping to shape the 20th century? Quite possibly, because H. G. Wells, who was a friend of Henry James for many years, published a book in 1915 called *Boon*, a satirical, anonymous novel in which he examined the literary lights around him with really sharp, precise, parody. And Henry James decided he'd had quite enough of this upstart who sold millions more books than he did. And Wells wasn't really capable of understanding his own motivations and this man who had helped to raise him as a writer, and so they had a fight. The literary world came down on the side of Henry James because it was after all, World War I, and science fiction was young, but science was killing people on the fields of France. Poison gas was invented by a Nobel Prize winning German chemist, etc., etc. World War I killed millions, millions. Not as may as the flu did, but almost. And they blamed science. Can't really blame humanity. You know, who shoots people? The guns or the people behind them? The literary people blamed the scientists to a great extent, and cut themselves away and we witnessed the birth of C. P. Snow's *The Two Cultures*, the separation between privileged upper classes who truly feared change, the academic classes who tended to espouse Marxism but adored upper-class literature . . . an incredible mix of antagonisms and contradictions arrayed against our nascent culture.

So we go back, circling back now, to where science fiction was left alone for a while to develop a new voice, a new flavor, a new rhythm, a new approach. A light approach in many cases. And not a particularly arrogant approach. We were not interested in style, and in many cases, character wasn't even particularly interesting. This was the literature of ideas. It was ideally suited to hit young people hard. Because young people don't really understand who people are either, they don't understand who they are, but ideas, visions, dreams and nightmares they get implicitly. It's what they're born to get. They feed off of them. So we were better than the Catholic church at converting the world. Because our dreams were bright dreams. Our hells were avoidable. We didn't have to do strange, ritualistic things to get out of the perils that we foresaw in the 21st century. Sometimes we could solve them with ballpoint pens and paper clips. What a vision: ingenuity. Brains, imagination and a sense of a loving appreciation of the life you are given was instilled through science fiction, injected into so many minds, including mine.

The histories written in the 21st century of the 20th century must include this and it will include examinations of the sociology of this; it will include examinations of how this all came to be in much the same way that people go back now and look at the origins of the Romantic movement and the poets and the brilliant geniuses who worked there. I was raised by you all in a really incredible time.

People will say that the golden age was the 1940s and 1950s, but Damon Knight is right; the golden age is 13. (laughter/applause)

So how do I pay it forward? I pay it forward by occasionally in a sane number of intervals over a number of years teaching at Clarion West and talking with incredible people who are now going forward and publishing their own books and, man, am I proud of that. I don't take credit for it, but you know, I had a little hand in it. I was there. A lot of the writers of my generation were there. We're doing a pretty good job. We're hitting the *New York Times* list; probably in a few years the *New York Times* will have to separate out the science fiction and fantasy list into its own list, which J. K. Rowling forced them to do.

The *New York Times* published an article on J. K. Rowling in which they said "We don't really understand where this woman came from, possibly from Tolkien . . . But you know," they said, rather approvingly, but grudgingly, "Bruno Bettelheim in the 1960s gave us the freedom to read fairy tales, so maybe this is all good after all." They seem to have missed *Star Wars*, and *Xena*, and Robert E. Howard and Conan and all the comic books and the *X-Men* and 10,000 movies and 10,000 TV shows which had set the stage for J. K. Rowling to come in and just sweep the audience away. Rowling did a good job, and you know what, she had fun. The audience had fun. We have fun. So let me end this on a quote that I've never actually confirmed, and if you like we can have some questions after.

Another very good author, John Barth, and someone correct me if they know the truth of this, but not right now. (laughter) John Barth said, "Science fiction writers. They are not like you and I. They have more fun."

Thank God for that! (Applause).